MEN BEHAVING BADLY

MEN

BEHAVING

BADLY

A NOVEL

SIMON NYE

HARPER & ROW, PUBLISHERS, New York
Cambridge, Philadelphia, San Francisco
1817 London, Mexico City, São Paulo, Singapore, Sydney

For Lucy

FIRST EDITION

Designed by Karen Savary

Library of Congress Cataloging-in-Publication Data
Nye, Simon, 1958–
  Men behaving badly.
  I. Title.
PR6064.Y44M46   1989   823'.914   88-45536
ISBN 0-06-016069-1

89 90 91 92 93 WB/HC 10 9 8 7 6 5 4 3 2 1

MEN BEHAVING BADLY

1st

"Blah blah blah blah blah blah blah blah blah."
"My God."
"Blah blah blah blah blah."
"God."
"Just on and on like that until I had to leave the room."
"Blah blah blah."
"That's it."
"You've told me this already."
"Are you sure?"
"You went on at some length the last time."
"I forget who I've told things to."
"Well don't."
"I just forget."
"*Don't* forget. When I repeat myself it's for emphasis. That's the only time. The *only* time."
"Did I say anything else about her?'"
"You gave a very full description, a range of similes."
"Teeth like stars."
"Nothing quite so old-fashioned."
"It was an education. To look so marvelous and be so dull."
"I know, you introduced me to her."
"No, it must have been someone else."
"It was definitely you. Dermot, I'm worried about your memory. Why are you pretending not to have one?"
"Don't worry about me. My brain is like a stiletto."

"Oh my God."

Dermot thrust back the chair with a false air of vigor and walked into the kitchen in his socks and his dressing gown.

"Blah blah drone drone incredible." He surveyed. "We're low on milk, low on butter, very low on bread. I'll tell you what, though."

"How low is very low?"

"We don't have any. I'll tell you what though. She looked absolutely memorable. I can see her now with the light on those bare shoulders she had."

"Dermot, you're droning."

"I can still picture the sweep of her hips," he shouted into the fluorescent interior of the fridge, where two different kinds of cheese sat effortlessly in the limelight.

In the café over the road Gary ordered a substantial breakfast of beans-bacon-mushrooms-tomato which had been done to a turn and then, unfortunately, done a bit longer. Dermot had a poached egg and a glance at the paper, which had nothing he hadn't seen before, the same squash of newsprint, the diurnal collage of mayhem. The atmosphere in the little room was close, so close there was hardly room for people. You had to cleave a space through the moist heat with your hands and shoulders.

Dermot folded his paper continentally into quarters and stuffed it into his pocket, trying to want to eat his egg but with no real hope of matching the overblown enthusiasm of the trenchermen who sat to his left and right, their massive thighs spilling over the sides of chairs.

"I prefer the cafés with the little old men lingering over their tea."

"What?"

"I don't like to see so much food early in the morning. And so much aggression."

"I don't know what you're talking about."

"Well look around you—breakfasts the size of briefcases, flashing bloody cutlery."

"You can't withdraw from the world, Dermot. I won't have it."

"You're more than usually lavish with advice this morning."

Gary leaned across the Formica, his beard close to his plate. "You're nervous aren't you."

"I *am* nervous."

"You've got egg around your mouth. Down a bit, under your lip. Now you've smeared it on your chin."

"Is it all off now?"

"You shouldn't have used your shirt cuff. It's one of the first things new employers look for, clean cuffs. Clean cuffs and nervelessness."

When it was all over they mopped down their mouths on the deltas of folded paper serviette, crunched them into dense white balls which opened up slowly like carnations on the plate, and paid on the way out. A facetious bell sealed their departure.

There were the usual two queues at the bus stop—one for the law-abiders with God on their side, the other for the rogues in the breakaway queue under the awning of the newsagents, waiting to slew across the pavement at the sight of the shimmering silhouette of a bus. Gary stood with these, Dermot with those. They had discussed it and come to a procedural deadlock—Dermot arguing for equity and democracy, Gary arguing for getting on the bus first.

A bus hove in through the lightening dawn and Gary swung himself aboard, leaving his associate to edge forward a place or two, nursing his moral superiority and a stomachful of resentment, again.

They had seen the training film, read the fire instructions, signed the forms. They were by now hoary old hands at the induction business.

Wheeled on from nowhere, however, a posse of brutal satirists reduced them nearly to tears over a torrid session of role-playing before lunch (Dermot was drawn to his group's instructress in some ways. He wasn't necessarily averse to discipline).

"Sonny. Do you call these shoes?"

"Has madam experienced problems with them?"

"They fell apart before my eyes."

"Before your eyes fell apart?"

"I didn't come here to be insulted."

"No, no. Much too easy. An old line."

Dermot was taken on one side and roughed up a little. He apologized elaborately and blamed his nerves. When he came back he did better.

"I've been waiting ten minutes to be served."

"I do apologize, madam. I was called away."

"This has never happened before."

"I am most dreadfully sorry."

"I've been coming here for years."

"We look forward to your visits."

"Look at the state of your cuffs. Get the manager."

"It's okay, he knows they've got shit on them."

He was taken on one side again and roughed up a little. The impression was given that the store was desperate for Christmas staff and Dermot's survival this far into the morning was proof of this desperation, this despair. He wasn't offended; he knew the games Personnel played, its cajoling attitude to new blood, its idiolect—tight ship, the customer is always, it is absolutely imperative that, and so on. Twenty-seven, he half suspected he was too old to be hearing these phrases. The others were all seventeen if they were a day and still young enough to knuckle down. Dermot didn't knuckle down any more.

Over lunch he talked to the youngsters over subsidized salad in the staff restaurant on the sixth floor, a self-consciously spartan aerie with seats of screechy plastic. They turned out to be not young at all, hardly a school leaver among them (although they had all, of course, left school at one time); the illusion was a feature of the lighting in the training department. There it was discreet, here it spoke in a loud voice much as Dermot did, throwing his views this way and that across the table, jabbing the air with his knife, fork and, afterwards, spoon. He was looking for a woman and his senses were painfully alive. New work and a set of new sexual tensions. He wanted to make his existence clear to the assembly, he wanted a profile so high it cast an endless shadow. The young lady in the check blouse like a tablecloth had cool smooth skin and a winning way with her slender mouth but she was taut with indifference, taut with it. The others noted Dermot's views civilly, with chimeral nods and frowns. The boys made boyish remarks about their uncomfortable suits and the girls said, No, I think a suit does something for a man.

Gary arrived at his shop and wrestled impatiently with the multiple locks. He was security conscious.

"George, can you help me with these fucking locks."

"Throw them all away and get yourself some insurance," George said, and helped him.

"Insurers are fat cats. I'd rather be robbed across the counter." The first padlock dislocated and the two men sighed and snorted and started on the second.

"Would you have a go?"

"How do you mean?"

"Have a go?"

"Have a go at what?"

"That's what they call it when you tackle a thief. Eighty-year-old sub-postmistress tackles intruder. Securicor man bites hand of man in balaclava."

"Is that the town in Russia or the woolly hat?"

The chain attached to the second padlock jangled substantially in the empty arcade where they plied their trade.

"There must be rust in the system. These keys, ancient—I suppose you think locksmiths are fat cats too."

"Fatter."

"I take it you wouldn't have a go, then."

"I might worry his ankles a bit, terrierlike, but I doubt it."

"Stamp dealer fails to make the effort. I don't like the sound of that."

"Philatelist shot dead making futile gesture. Anyway I have a little insurance—I believe it was called the safety net policy and seemed to be made up entirely of exclusions. To get any money I have to be burgled by lepers during a full moon."

"You want to watch those exclusions."

"This is what I'm saying."

Gary finally threw off his chains and left them curled on the floor like a bad case of colic. He pushed up the shutter, which clattered edgily to the ceiling, and let the accumulation of stale, papery air slip past him and to freedom. George went back to the adjoining stall and fell on the remains of his breakfast—half a paper cup of tea and the stub of a banana. Gary could tell from the sound of George swallowing down the tea like a pelican and the wet downfall of the banana skin as it missed the bin. Gary clicked on the light and shuffled through his hefty doughnut of keys (he jingled wherever he went) for the gnarled machine which unlocked the safe. Inside, everything was as he had left it—not unreasonably, since it was a safe and therefore kept locked during the night. The litany of noises continued for some minutes—the cashbox being hauled across the floor of the safe, the heavy door gasping on its hinges, the roulettish twirl of the combination—and then he sat down on his plump chair to count the money, watching the arrival of his dealer colleagues and rivals. Some wore stiff city gray, others modeled floppy cardigans knitted, apparently, with someone else in mind. Gary paid out greetings, or was greeted.

"Hello. Cold one."

"Hello." And then, more formally.

"Good morning."

"Morning. Cold one."

They must be referring to the weather.

"New coat, Peter."

"Barathea."

"No, I said new coat, Peter."

"Coat, yes. Brrr!"

It was a male environment and they had their clubby satisfactions. Gary was almost the youngest and, twenty-seven, far too young to be talking about the weather. He had already met his trading partners halfway by agreeing to talk to them at all. You had to, in effect, if you wanted to make a go of selling stamps. He had a reputation as a hard man and the upkeep of this reputation made him weary at times. Young men in this business, he realized, could choose to be callow sadists or bumblers in slippers. George, for example, had just slipped into his plaid mules.

"Did I tell you I was robbed once?" George said through the thin dividing wall.

"No you never told me that."

"I was doing a summer season in Torquay."

"You *are* a dark horse. What did you do—Punch and Judy, alternative cabaret?"

"I sold stamps."

"Not very visual."

"It was quiet up here and my wife suggested we take a stall on the English Riviera. That's what they call Torquay now."

"I rather liked the name Torquay."

"So I said yes, why not have a go."

"You mean you tackled the intruder."

"No, I agreed to spend a month or two at the seaside." George was not troubled with a sense of humor. His detection rate for irony was barely into double figures. "I did tackle him in fact, but I was a bit too psychological."

"How do you mean too psychological, George?"

"I tried to talk him out of it."

"You got him to talk about his mother, you encouraged him to recreate some trauma."

"No, I was jocular."

"Jocular."

"I tried to make him relax and put away his knife. I offered him the 1965 Christmas set from Ascension Island."

"Pretty stamps—a shrewd move."

7

"But he wanted money."

"You should have tried something flashier, Tongan triangulars, wildlife in Sierra Leone."

"My mind wasn't working clearly."

"Still, you got it back on the insurance."

"No. I didn't want to lose my no claims bonus."

Gary wanted to stop the conversation at this point but it had a momentum of its own.

"I thought that was just for cars and motorbikes."

"That's not what I was told."

"What would it take before you claimed money, then? I mean what is the point otherwise. I should think they were laughing behind their hands down at the brokers. That's the trouble with the insurance industry—it's dealing with criminals the whole time, car thieves, bent Spanish trawler magnates. It's bound to rub off on their own mentality. Like policemen. It's the stink of corruption, you see George—it doesn't waft selectively, it pervades. How much did you lose?"

"Four shillings and sixpence."

"I see."

Dermot was footsore as he made it to the front door and stuck his Yale home. He didn't want to speak to anyone for two or three hours. It was inevitable, therefore, that Geraldine should be waiting for him beyond the stippled glass, just two or three hours too early.

"Dermot you look tired, love."

"I started a new job today."

"How super!"

He put his foot on the first of the stairs that led to the safety of his own flat.

"I have an announcement to make!" She was effervescent. "A young lady's moving in upstairs."

"Can we talk about it later, Geraldine. I have to go and sit in a chair."

"She's a pretty little thing."

"You mean she'll need a hand with her suitcases."

8

He apologized for his brusqueness, brusquely, and went gently up the stairs.

Gary had a headache as he reached the front door (a birthday cake of pink gloss and frosting) and sheathed one of his many keys in the mortise. The first day of November had been peppered with spiteful moments—he had spilt coffee not once but twice over pages of stamps, he had been called a "greedy young man," he had been visited by feelings of personal inadequacy. Geraldine's body loomed distortedly through the crazed prisms of the door, which Gary opened with a heavy heart.

"Hello love. You're looking a little tense."

"I know."

"All those itsy-bitsy stamps—you should be out in the fresh air."

"The itsy-bitsy stamps would blow away." She produced a heavy-duty laugh and rounded it off with a cockeyed smile.

"I have an announcement to make!"

"I'm ready." Her body *was* distorted, actually. Gary could see that now.

"A young lady's moving in upstairs tomorrow. I think you're going to like her."

"All that I ask is that she's light on her feet. The last one clog-danced into the early hours. And she dropped objects the whole time, on our ceiling."

"Oh, you are a monkey!" she squealed and tickled his ribs.

"I'm a monkey am I," he sighed, and moved ponderously up the stairs.

"She's a pretty little thing," she called after him.

"Well I'm sure Dermot will help her with her suitcases."

2 nd

Geraldine was the proprietor-landlady. She was of a certain age, and the certain age was fifty-one (Gary knew because he had celebrated two birthdays with her and the fiftieth had not been a picnic, let him tell you that, let him make that quite plain. She had got through a fair amount of wailing because, she said, fifty sounds so old, so very very old. Collaring him or Dermot on staircases, in the porch, by the front gate, she shared with them her dread of the awesome milestone. In the end they more or less had to tell her to pull herself together). She had a husband who was an altogether less dynamic person than herself and it was he, they guessed from his footfall, who had pushed the note under the door. The house style, however, was hers.

> Boys, I'm having a little supper.
> Come along and meet Deborah! I've
> invited Gwen so there. Seven o'clock.

Dermot fingered the piece of paper. "What does Deborah say to you, Gary?"

He stared into his black morning coffee. "Many things. It says Jewish parents. Or her father was a big fan of Debbie Reynolds. My father wanted to call me Debbie for the same reason."

"It would have been character-building for you."

"Not as much as my mother's choice—Bing."

"I meant her physical appearance."

10

"I'm not interested."

"How is Dorothy? You don't bring her home as much as you used to. I take it she's the reason for your lack of interest."

"I don't look at girls anymore. I don't even look at Dorothy anymore."

"But you still see her."

"Out of the corner of my eye. You should try to lose your obsession with sex."

"It's not an obsession, Gary. It's written into my genes."

"Write it out, Dermot. I have whiteout."

It was true. If Dermot's mind was a wheel (it wasn't a wheel) sex was its shiny hub, he sometimes thought, and everything else flew centrifugally away. He had another metaphor: His life was a journey and the women in it were places he visited. They might leave him but it always seemed to be him that moved on while they stood still. Bye-bye Beverly and Dollis Hills. Victoria falls and then Georgia's on my mind.

"As I see it," Dermot said, "we are all animals. I am an animal."

"And I am an animal, then."

"That's right."

"Where does that get us? You have no idea about setting up a cogent argument—you just wield these portentous phrases like a two-bit politician. So I'm an animal."

"Don't get angry."

"Geraldine said I was a monkey yesterday."

"I'm sure she didn't mean it."

"Well of course she didn't fucking mean it. That's twice it's happened in twenty-four hours, that's all I'm saying."

Dermot felt bad about the milk situation, another euphemism he used for *not having any milk*. He had forgotten to buy any the day before. It was his turn. So he felt bad. They should get it delivered. There was no food either.

"I'm sorry about the shoddy breakfast this morning. I was too tired to go shopping."

"I wouldn't call it shoddy. A little astringent, perhaps, just a cup of black coffee." He got up. "See you tonight, animal."

11

Dermot sat back on his chair, shut his eyes and waited for the day to be over.

When it was, the evening began. It was a Friday but Dermot and Gary both had to work the following day, so their Friday evening could not be like the Friday evening of some young guns, who drank themselves into oblivion and lurched home with their heads heavy on their necks and their stomachs drying on their shoes. They did that on other evenings, the drinking and the lurching. They liked a night out, Dermot and Gary, although not so much Gary, who easily preferred a night in. After a period of experimentation they had reached a compromise—many evenings Dermot would go out *on his own* and Gary would stay at home. Tonight's arrangement was another smart compromise—eating out without leaving the comfort of their front door, in other words eating with their landlord and -lady.

"Hello Geraldine."

"Darling you've brought some wine. But we already have a bottle."

Dermot had not often eaten in Geraldine's downstairs flat and he had forgotten that she thought one bottle of wine was enough for the evening.

"Well you have it another time."

"Christmas, perhaps."

"A good idea."

"I heard on the radio this morning that there were only a certain number of shopping days left till Christmas."

"And the nights have really drawn in," *ohdearohdear,* thought Dermot.

"I think Christmas is terribly overcommercialized, don't you?" This was Gary, appearing at the door. "But I suppose that's nothing more than a cliché really."

"Flowers. You are a dear."

"I believe they're your favorite kind."

"Yellow ones, absolutely! I'll put them in water and open a tin or two."

The two of them stood in the middle of her living room, alone. Dermot was in his work suit and looked like he had slept in it, turbulently, while Gary wore a pair of new jeans and a bright new sweater and, aiming to look casual, looked as casual as a lighthouse. They started to walk vaguely about the room, moving from one item of interest to another. Dermot fastened onto the trinkets on the mantlepiece. He shook the Eiffel Tower in its bubble and watched the snow fall. He picked up a flamboyant ashtray and read Aloha from Hawaii (what was it, this Aloha?). The white china horse he did not touch for fear of breaking it, because it was precariously prancing on its hind legs. She returned.

"I didn't know you'd been to Hawaii, Geraldine."

"I haven't," she replied, which did not explain the ashtray. She put down the vase of flowers and went back to the kitchen shouting, "A few more tins and I'll be with you."

Gary had wedged one hand into his crisp, overwhelmingly snug jeans and looked less casual than ever. He was by the bookshelf, thoroughly approving of the paucity of books and with the other hand activating a snow-bubble with a Roman villa and a kneeling figure inside it. Setting it on the shelf to watch, Gary was perplexed by the redness of the waterborne snow until he realized this was meant to be Vesuvius raining down on Pompeii. Quite the best toy, in his opinion, since the dog with the broken neck that nods in cars. Geraldine had an affection for these devices, that much was clear. There were at least a dozen scattered around the room and Gary imagined her darting around the homely interior shaking one after the other to keep them all on the go at once, like a circus plate-spinner. People get up to the strangest things, after all, when the curtains are drawn.

The rattle of food arguing its way out of tins was heard in the kitchen.

"Shall we offer to help?"

"It might be a good idea."

Geraldine had a tube of kidney beans between her clenched thighs and was straining to turn the great butterfly of the tin opener. Gary took over on the butterfly and he and Dermot peeled a lot of very small potatoes at the sink, while their hostess looked on in her cranky fashion.

"Where's the new lodger, then?" Dermot eventually asked, his manners blunted by his time at the sink.

"There's been a hitch," she said.

"She's let you down."

"Calm down, Dermot."

"No, she's coming but she may be late. Darlings, you're doing a fine, fine job. I'm not used to having young men in my kitchen."

"Where's Gerald?"

Gerald was coming through the door. Nobody said Talk of the Devil but it hung in their mouths like a burden.

"Traffic," he said.

"It's not real, is it," his wife agreed.

"Yes," he said, and went to change. Since an accident at work many years earlier, Gerald's powers of speech had been impaired. He had been working at the information desk in the National Gallery when an attendant had been struck a glancing blow from a badly hung Constable and rendered unconscious by the gilt immensity of its frame. Due to a rostering crisis no immediate replacement was available and Gerald was ushered in to fill the breach since he had no pride when it came to job demarcation. They rehung the Constable, warned Gerald not to stand too close to the wall until the other mountings had been checked (or on his own head be it) and sent him out among the paintings. He got a taste for the standing around, the uniform, and not having to say anything for hours on end, and refused to be moved back to Information when the roster and the concussed functionary were finally straightened out.

Gary and Dermot had talked about this and come to no particular conclusions. Gerald had said less and less, apparently, since the day he embarked on this silent, watchful vocation. Few tourists asked him anything and when they did he pointed, apparently, or nodded or used his hands expressively.

14

He seemed to be retreating inside his own head and Dermot had a tentative theory that the paintings were to blame. He had worked in a gallery himself and had become mesmerized by the ominous rectangles. These shapes of smeared oil carried so much more weight than the visitors to the gallery, who shuffled and slunk from painting to painting and room to room leaving nothing behind them but the smell of the outside world, their evaporating commentaries ("Hey, look at those greens!") and the memory of their softly crackling carrier bags. The pictures remained, stuck to the walls and serious about being there. But, but. It was fine art but was it healthy art? Dermot sometimes drew up close to look at the paintings. It was difficult to find a connection between the human hand and these congealed and venerable brushstrokes. There was more that was dead than alive about the paintings he watched over. What kind of art ever came in a frame, smoothed down and shuttered into two dismal dimensions? Maybe Gerald could learn from Dermot, whose special interest among the arts was in modern ballet, although in practice he would settle for go-go dancing.

Alternatively Gerald may simply have been infected by quietness (although librarians, of course, normally acquire over the years voices that carry to the end of the universe) or he may always have been a silent person struggling inside a louder one, waiting to burst out and proclaim, whisperingly or on a scribbled note, that he was giving up speaking.

Whatever had happened, Gerald was now as much use at dinner parties as a dog in a supermarket.

After a while Geraldine went away, leaving Dermot and Gary to struggle with the potatoes, which were small, knuckly and gray and should have been plowed back into the field.

"Good day at work?" Dermot asked.

"I don't want to talk about it. Can I try your peeler?"

"What kind of household has two peelers?" Dermot said as he swapped. "It's not an indulgence I would ever allow myself."

"His and hers."

"I can understand that for towels and toilets but surely not kitchen implements."

"Joking, Dermot. I was joking."

"Although some things strike me as very feminine."

"Pencil skirts, long hairs in the bath, sitting with your knees together..."

"No, *things*. A spoon, for example?"

"Feminine."

"An egg timer."

"Well, obviously."

"And there are the masculine objects. Toast rack, steak mallet, pressure cooker—No, not the pressure cooker."

"Have you been working in the Kitchenware department, Dermot? This is a stupid conversation."

"Yes I have. It's in the basement if you want to come and see me in action. They said they try to fit our characters to what we sell."

"Do they *sell* dickheads in your shop?"

Having been left on their own, they went ahead and cooked the meal. With a certain amount of nervousness, because they had been given no instructions, they decided to boil the potatoes and tip the kidney beans into the saucepan that gently seethed and wheezed on the cooker. Gary was all for herbs but Dermot thought they should wait until a host reappeared.

After a while noises started to come from the bedroom. Most of them were the sounds of a woman, frustrated cries, and although they were muffled by the time they reached the kitchen, they were obviously very loud when they left Geraldine's chords and mobile mouth. A period of calm followed but then, as the potatoes began to soften and the stew to writhe, bloated and ready, the shouting started again. It was impossible to know what it was about because the few phrases they heard had lost all their syntactical logic in the turmoil of the argument. A door slammed and then a door more distant still. Gerald had fled, leaving his wife in the bedroom where

Gary guessed she was pummeling the counterpane with her bony fists. He made no movement towards her room in case she was still explosive, and Dermot, too, went on laying the kitchen table. In due course Geraldine left as well, trotting on her audibly pointy heels down the garden path and through the space where the gate used to be.

"Was she crying?"

"I think so."

"She's gone after him."

"I know. I'm going to add some chili powder and a clove of garlic."

"Okay."

They ate together in the ill-lit kitchen, sharing the table with a lonely geranium and a cluster of supernumerary cutlery. They switched the radio on, for company, and cleaned their plates to the sound of the Northern Radio Orchestra and the BBC Singers. Gwen, Geraldine's friend from next door, had failed to appear and so had Deborah, whose name was now synonymous with mystery and unreliability. Gwen's failure to arrive had been the biggest success of the evening and they toasted her absence in wine.

They drank the bottle slowly, washed the twin-set of crockery, turned off the radio and a few of the lights and went to the door, leaving the smell-haze of food behind them.

As they padded up the stairs the front door opened and Gerald entered lugubriously, his wife at his heel.

"Night, boys."

"Night, Gerald."

"Night Gerald, Geraldine."

"Night, boys."

"Night, Geraldine."

3rd

A loud knock on the door woke Gary up. It was still dark beyond the curtains and it was dark inside the room until he focused on the legend of his electronic alarm clock, which glowed red on black like an usherette's torch. It was a dark knock, too, as if the door was being struck low down with the toe of a despairing shoe. He lay on an arm and dwelt for a moment on the two compelling facts—it was 6:40 and somebody wanted him to open the door. 6:41. Time was moving. 6:42. Hark at those shuffling minutes.

He found his dressing gown on the door and put it on, making sure the folds hung down smart and parallel and the ends from the loose bow of his belt were equal in length over the mound of his stomach. Ready.

The knocking had stopped but Gary walked through the hall and opened the door.

"Can I help?" he called down the stairs.

"Yes."

He went back for a pair of stout brown shoes and laced them neatly over his shivering white feet. He felt bottom-heavy with them on and was conscious of the two shafts of cold leg between his shoes and his knee-length gown, but he went ahead and walked towards the voice at the bottom of the stairs.

"Ah," he said. "I see your problem."

"I need help with this case."

"Trunk. It's actually a trunk."

"Yes, I suppose it is. I've had it for years."

"I'm not sure I can manage it on my own. Have you asked Gerald to help?"

"He gave me the key and went back to bed. It's difficult for a woman on her own."

"It must be."

"I know it's early."

"It doesn't matter. I'm sure you had your reasons."

"No. I just wanted to come."

She was sitting on the trunk, looking very composed. Her blond hair was short and her cheeks pink, from both the chill of the morning and the rosy brocade of the lightshade. He didn't like to ask too many questions yet, but he wondered for a start if she dyed her hair. She had dark eyebrows but body hair was from all accounts a bad guide and perhaps she dyed her eyebrows.

"It's got handles, hasn't it?"

"Yes. Strong handles."

"Right."

"I thought there were two of you upstairs. Why not get your friend to help? The taxi driver had a lot of trouble bringing it this far."

Surprising himself, Gary replied, "I'd rather not disturb him. He's a pig in the morning."

"I suppose I could leave it here."

"Risky."

"That's what I thought."

"You've had it for years, after all. It would be a shame if it was stolen."

He tightened the knot round his waist and she jumped daintily from the trunk to smooth her flat frame against the wall. Gary squeezed past, smelling no perfume on her raincoated body, and fitted his hand weightlifter-like around the handle. It moved easily at first, sliding on the impoverished nap of the hall carpet, but he had intimations of difficulty and suffering when he started to drag it up the stairs' slippery scarp. With back bent double, his chest on his knees, Gary tried not to topple forward. He rested on the first bend.

"I've done a lot of shifting in my time," he said hoarsely. He was aware that his thighs had been showing and he regretted their pallor.

On the landing they took another break. Gary sat on the trunk this time. He alluded to the building of Stonehenge and the Pyramids while Deborah leant on the banister.

The stairs narrowed now and he decided to push. The metal edge of the trunk was cold on his hands and then on his chest when he laid it there, between the gaping lapels of the dressing gown, the belt of which had freed itself. His absurdly polished shoes glinted up at him as he clutched the beast and he felt her eyes on his exposed underpants.

"Good."

"Where would you like it?" He was gasping.

"Under the window, if you're sure it won't kill you."

He wasn't, but he put it there anyway.

"Let me make you some tea." She unbelted her dark blue raincoat which reminded Gary of one he used to wear at school, and revealed another, khaki one which she also removed. "It was easier than carrying it." He switched on the electric fire and she went through three cardboard boxes before she found a box of teabags, two mugs, a kettle, a box of matches and a spoon.

"How's your back? I thought I heard it crack back there on the stairs."

"It must have been a floorboard," he answered. It had been his back.

"How long have you been living here? The lady seemed very fond of you."

"A couple of years. She expected you yesterday, you know."

"Yes, I had trouble with my boyfriend. He kept unpacking my bags."

"Men can be very unreasonable. How did you get away in the end?"

"He had to go away for the weekend. I've finished with him." She turned back to the gas ring and silenced the whistling kettle. Her movements were measured and efficient under the gray tracksuit, which was smooth over her busy body. "There's no milk, I'm afraid." She handed over the mug and sat opposite Gary on the floor. He was not the kind of person, in his opinion, who was at his best in these informal positions.

"I'm quite happy with it black."

She didn't smile much, but had a very open face, small nose. After each swallow of tea her lower lip came up over the upper one and wiped it gently. Gary found the gesture childlike but couldn't remember if he had ever seen it on a child.

"You must be Deborah."

"You must be Gary."

"How did you guess?"

"It says so on your dressing gown."

"Oh yes. It was an offer—free name or initials with every garment. I chose the name because it had more letters."

"Uh huh."

"Yup."

"Uh huh."

A silence fell between them while outside the sun rose. Gary hurried to put away his tea because he didn't want to be late for work. Saturday was his busiest day.

"I have to go now," he said, with great ceremony, "but you must come round this evening."

There were so many people in Dermot's shop that he wanted to hide in one of the department's freezers until they all left at the end of the day. He wanted to curl up in the largest of the spin driers and reduce their noise to the level of a rumor.

"Excuse me can you tell me the way to the 'ladies'?"

"Pardon? You'll have to shout."

"Where is the 'ladies'?"

21

"You mean where *are* the ladies." She was a confused old lady but Dermot couldn't let her get away with bad grammar. "Well there are a lot over there in the microwave section and quite a few watching the Magipeel demonstration. You really can't move for them." She obviously couldn't hear him above the flurry of the shop floor and had walked away on her unsteady legs. Dermot hated his attitude.

"Young man. Do you have any coffee mugs?"

"We've got five."

"Only five?"

"And a couple of those are chipped. We keep meaning to get some more but you know how it is, you keep putting off the moment."

"I can't believe it. In a shop this size."

"Oh *sorry*. I thought you meant at home."

Dermot had a big headache and couldn't follow what people were saying. The basement had a low ceiling, unlike the ground floor which seemed to have no ceiling at all it was so high. They had a carpet upstairs but down here they had no carpet. The checkered lino was hard on his feet and on his eyes.

"Hey mate. Have you got one of those things for..."

"For what?"

"I'm trying to remember. You know, it's flat at the bottom."

"Fridge?"

"No, no. Smaller. The wife uses it on the clothes."

"I can see you're not domesticated, if I may say so sir. Sewing machines are Haberdashery, third floor."

"No, watch." The man started on a charade, making hissing noises and steering his arm through the air.

"Ah, soda syphon! You confused me when you mentioned clothes."

"No, I've got it. Steam iron!"

"We're out of stock."

If it was going to be this hectic every Saturday Dermot would have to arrange a series of dental appointments or a sick mother who had to be visited every weekend all weekend, less she die of loneliness. It was the pre-Christmas rush, apparently, and followed on each year from the autumn boom. The actual Christmas rush was due in a week or two and would in its turn be superseded by the Sale Madness of the New Year. If Dermot was going to excuse himself for dental appointments it would have to be for a whole mouth he was having installed bit by bit—a grandiose and exhausting lie. Maybe if he just stood it out he would learn to get through until half past five, when the last voice retired up the escalator and left him and his colleagues to a momentary peace among the appliances.

Gary was in the supermarket. He had left his stamp shop an hour early. Heartbreaking. Customers had still been milling and looking eager to spend. He had to get to the shops before they shut. The trouble with late Saturday shopping, he was discovering, was that although the doors were open there was a lot of nothing on the shelves. Where had it all gone? In the meat fridge he found nothing but two sheep's hearts and a packet of turkeyburgers. Whenever he came in for a jar of coffee and a packet of biscuits the place would be stacked up with chickens, clogged with offal and thick red muscle. Not today when he needed precisely that.

He wheeled his trolley down the aisle. There was a party atmosphere in the haggard interior of the shop—a poor party, finishing. Gary was the late arrival. His trolley squeaked. He had decided to take the hearts and the burgers and now chose vegetables with the speed and purpose of a man with no mind. He was eventually manhandled through the checkout and the glass doors by the remaining staff.

Geraldine met him in the hall. She must have been loitering there.

"I *am* sorry about last night. I told Gwen the wrong evening."

"Don't you worry," said Gary affably, "we had the time of our lives. Excuse me, but I have to entertain this evening."

"I don't know what's come over him."

"You must mean Gerald."

23

"Yes, Gerald."

"I shouldn't worry. We can't act normally all the time. By the law of averages somebody somewhere is always giving someone else a bad time."

"But it's always *me*, darling. I am that someone else."

"Oh hardly. It rotates. Anyway it was a lovely meal and I hope the two of you sort things out over the weekend." It was a parting shot but she kept him there.

"Talk to him. Ask him if he's seeing another woman."

"Ask him yourself. How long have you been married?"

"Twenty-nine years."

"Well then."

"Well then what?"

"You must know how to talk to him."

"I've known my mother over fifty years and I don't say a word to her."

"Your personalities probably clash."

"That's exactly it. You obviously have a feeling for these things."

"I really have to go upstairs. Have a word with Dermot about it. He's had a lot of affairs."

Geraldine burst into tears and the sobs were awful to see. Gary gathered her bony arms in his fleshy arms and stood uneasily with her head on his chest until the sobs smoothed themselves away. The clinch was interrupted by Gerald, arriving.

"Hello Gary."

"Hello Gerald. I was just comforting your wife."

"Right you are."

Gary was low, Dermot was high. Both were working hard.

In the bedrooms Dermot was sucking at the carpet with a Hoover, shimmying among the legs of beds. He had an apron on and a scarf tied round his head like a pantomime cleaner, to show he was in a good mood, a festive mood. Gary had thought he was going out and here he had made a mistake. He was staying in. Deborah was coming to eat, or so it seemed, so he was staying. Gary was cooking sheep's hearts and he didn't buy something as unusual as that if he was entertaining the back of a bus.

Gary was wiping surfaces in the kitchen. He had a cloth and a bowl and kept discovering new surfaces. He was always a fastidious hygienist—ever since school when he had the only pencil case that always smelt of antiseptic, the only locker without a resinous stain or a radioactive apple core. But at that moment he was too disheartened by Dermot's refusal to *get the hell out* as he always did on Saturday nights (he was constantly bragging that he needed to *get the hell out* on a Saturday night and go wild to a certain extent) that he cleaned badly, without going right into the corners.

"Why have you stopped Hoovering?" he yelled.

"I'm readjusting my headscarf."

"Dermot?"

"Yes?"

"Get back to that Hoovering."

"Don't put pressure on me."

The noise began again and the theme tune of Desert Island Discs was drowned by its breathy resonance.

"Deborah. Pleased to meet you, my name's Dermot. Dermot by name, Dermot by nature."

She was casually dressed and smiled politely.

"Deborah," she said succinctly. "I've come from upstairs."

"You certainly have!" Of course, he was a bit nervous. "I gather you met Gary this morning. He's in the kitchen. I usually answer the door."

"So do I," she said. Dermot creased his face and indulged in a small amount of laughter.

"How are you settling in?"

"Very well."

"Let me take your coat."

"I'm not wearing one."

"I understand. I expect you'll want to keep that tracksuit on. Come through. Let me introduce you to Gary."

They walked through to the kitchen.

"Ah. Hello Deborah. Deborah, meet Dermot. Dermot, Deborah."

"Hello, Dermot. Actually we met in the hall when he answered the door."

"How are you settling in?"

"It's quite hard work. I have a lot of silly little things to unpack."

"That's not what you told me in the hall," Dermot said.

The men laughed recklessly.

"I hope you're not a vegetarian," Gary said when they were quiet again.

"Not at all."

"You have to ask nowadays. You can't always tell from the way people look."

"I don't drink alcohol, though. People assume you always do unless you tell them you don't."

"We both do drink, I'm afraid, but Dermot can't take too much."

"The truth is that after Gary's had two glasses of wine he becomes very excitable and has to go straight home to bed."

"My father was an alcoholic."

"Oh, I am sorry," the men said together.

"It's alright. He's not dead."

"It was insensitive."

"Not really."

"I suppose not. I mean, he could have been a publican or run an off-license."

"He was, he did. Most publicans are alcoholics."

"I can believe it," said Dermot, anxious not to get left behind in the brittle dialogue. "It's like doctors and drug addiction, miners and pneumoconiosis." He paused and sighed. "Men and women" he added, dying.

They took Deborah on a tour of the flat, starting with the kitchen. They pointed out the cooker, the sink and the clean work surfaces. Gary took advantage of his extra height to show her the electricity meter in its high little cupboard. She was impressed with the kitchen, or she said she was. And so it went with the hall and bathroom but they hesitated on the threshold of the bedrooms, conscious that here the smallest details make large differences. Dermot had a Popeye alarm clock. He was slightly worried about that. Popeye's massive forearms worked round and the alarm bell crashed between two spinach cans. Irony, he had heard, traveled badly and this was an ironic clock.

Gary was worried about Deborah's reaction to his single bed. He had always meant to buy a double; he saw now that this refusal to buy was his last stand against adulthood, just as some men never gave up warm milk. Living with mother. Sleeping with the light on. In spite of his bulk he was agile in bed and hardly ever fell out in company, but how could he explain this to Deborah? She would consider him sexless, simply because of his facilities.

"You're tidy."

"My parents were tidy before me." It was not what he wanted to be known for, tidiness. And then suddenly he was off and wondering why, why, why do I care so much? She had pretty blond hair which, incidentally, made a herringbone descent down her spine from her nape—those soft, intimate hairs sensitive men always talk about when in conversation with other sensitive men. She had all that, and she had that same gray tracksuit, loose limbs and a clean, clear voice, but Gary was making no sense to himself. This was not enough. He decided to see to it that he would no longer hang on her lips, like a mere boy.

"Yes," he blurted, "it's a single bed. I keep meaning to get a double but, you know, I really can't be bothered. And being so tidy I sleep tidily, of course."

"And this must be Dermot's room...."

Dermot had the turkeyburgers, the others had heart. He did not read anything symbolic into this, though he noted the symbolism.

He loved Deborah and he could tell you why. There was no mystery. People like Gary created mysteries because their bloodless lives needed fleshing out with internal doubts and games. Dermot knew it was a question of geometry—Deborah had the angles, arcs and planes that were right for him. She held her head the way he liked. The swivel of her hips corresponded to his idea of an impeccable swivel. She had a state-of-the-art Cleopatran nose. But although her geometry was perfect for him (it really was a good system) it was not a universal standard. Deborah was small and there were those that insisted on big. Her breasts were also small and there were many men that were only happy with big breasts, or they were happy with small breasts but only on a tall girl, or they wanted virtually no breast at all. Some men didn't care what they had and they usually ended up with nothing, their desires too diffuse. Dermot had made this mistake in the past. He was okay now. He knew what he wanted.

4th

Both Dermot and Gary were religious. Every Sunday they religiously took part in some kind of sport together. In the summer they had played cricket but now, in autumn, they did something different every week. Gary preferred ball games and tests of strength, while Dermot specialized in endurance and preparing the flask of soup.

"Have you brought the soup?"

"It's in the bag."

"What flavor?"

"I can't remember. It's got bits floating in it."

"Minestrone?"

"No, I don't think it was minestrone."

"You forgot to buy a newspaper."

"It was a decision. I haven't been enjoying the news lately."

"It's what I've said all along. Paying good money to read about bad and sad things."

"There are humorous articles."

"I hate that shitty word, *humorous*. I keep hearing it on the radio. *Humorous.*"

Gary looked down at the shopfronts as they slipped by. He always sat next to the window and when he didn't want to talk he watched the street life. It was a different crowd on Sundays. There were churchgoers and far more dogs, and the kids really did hang around on street corners. They chose the corners, Gary supposed, because that gave them a view down at least two streets; if you were doing nothing more than hanging around it made good sense to choose a corner.

Gary's low mood had slept with him and was still there in the morning. He had been thinking of calling Dorothy. His knees were pressing into the seat in front—he only ever noticed this when he was dejected. Until he cheered up or got off the bus, Gary's knees would be at the forefront of his mind, alongside his melancholy. And he was not looking forward to running around the park. He had wanted to play squash but something had gone wrong with his powers of persuasion and Dermot would not waive his right to choose.

"You know those bits—what color were they?"

"What?"

"Were they yellow like noodles or all different?"

"Does it really matter?"

"Of course it doesn't matter."

"Look, next week you make the soup."

"Don't be so bloody childish."

Dorothy was probably what he needed. He knew he ought to treat her better. Recently he had made her angry by telling her a scurrilous joke. "Dorothy," he had said, "what's the difference between a woman and a toilet?" They had been enjoying themselves more than usual that evening and he had spoilt it all.

"Dermot," he now said, "what's the difference between a woman and a toilet?"

"I don't want to know."

"A toilet doesn't follow you around after you've used it."

"That's a disgusting thing to say."

"Just what Dorothy said. I think she meant it more than you, though."

"You're so tactless."

"I don't *mean* it. Anyway a woman told me it, I just switched the genders."

"I don't believe you. You don't know any women."

"Alright, but I could quite easily have heard it from a

woman. They don't sit around telling jokes about Tupperware, you know. Not anymore."

They got off the bus and walked under the elaborate wrought-iron arch into the park. The path was treacherous with dead leaves marinating in tarmac pools. Dermot swung the bag containing the flask and looked around at the wet scenery. Gary's eyes were slitted against the low sun and his hands felt cold. They walked past a stack of clammy wood and leaves which was fodder for the civic bonfire the following day. A small boy was guarding it self-consciously. Last year someone had set fire to it a day early.

The weather was bright and a few people were out, feeding the obese pigeons, walking or wheeling their children. Gary would have loved to be wheeled.

"What shall we do about the bag?" he asked.

"Leave it with someone."

"I don't trust anyone enough."

"What about that old lady over there? I don't think we'll get much trouble out of her."

"We'd have to share the soup with her afterwards. Old people live on soup."

"Alright we'll leave it behind a tree."

"I'd rather leave it with the old lady."

However, when they started to strip off their clothes to reveal their shorts she scuttled away. They sat on the moist bench for a while feeling the air on their legs and then, duly leaving the bag behind a tree, they ran off like freed animals.

Gary was more conscious of their absurdity than Dermot, who in any case looked less absurd than he. Dermot was a gazelle and his legs cut the air incisively with a high action that brought his thighs almost parallel with the ground, whereas Gary's shuffled through vertically, grudgingly. And yet he was not one to collapse at the first ache in his side. He was not a joke. He did it to stay young but it made him feel old. But there was pleasure to be had even in the discredited madness of running through parks; Gary was much happier to run now that

31

the dangers were so well-documented—the shattered joints, bleeding toes and nipples. It was more dangerous, medically, than falling down a mountain, was the implication.

The park had undulations which tested the resilience of their legs and their concentration. They ran along the touch-lines of football games, where anoraked figures shouted in broken sentences at their galley slaves or heroes on the pitch. These people were a distraction, with their grisly exhortations and mindless enthusiasm. There was even a game of women's hockey which the two men turned to watch. Gary saw the rosy, mottled meat of their splattered thighs and turned away, but Dermot's eyes watched as long as possible until the ladies were lost behind a dune of wet grass.

Breath had to be fought for now. Gary was nearly out of it, because his chest told him so. Dermot looked ashen and Gary knew his own face was red; he had seen them once together in the squash club mirror, he ripe and hot-looking in the afterglow of the game, his body boiling inside with spent but undissipated energy, while Dermot sat with gray sunken cheeks and pale green gills. Gary's own redness was particularly marked on his forehead because most of his cheeks and chin was lagged in a dense black beard which squeezed the heat out through the top of his face.

"Can we stop?" They stopped.

"Why?"

"It's better when you break it up," Gary said. It was hard to talk standing up so he lay down on his back.

"Where did you read that?"

"I just made it up."

"It's best to keep going until you feel pain. You'll get stiff lying there."

"I don't mind stiff."

Dermot lay down next to Gary. Both of them wanted to talk about Deborah, and the euphoria of exhaustion brought their suppressed desires to the surface.

"What did you think about last night? I thought it went well."

"I thought it went well. She's a lovely girl."

"Dermot, you say that about them all. The words have no meaning."

"No, really. She's a lovely girl. Don't you think she is?"

"I don't rush in with my judgments. I give my opinions time to ferment."

"I'll tell you what you do. You make your judgments, or rather they are made on your behalf—chemistry, biology—"

"Yeah, yeah."

"Memory, glands—these do the deciding and then a week or two later or maybe a month you decide to cough up the stale old news."

"Ah, but that decision was also taken on my behalf—chemistry, biology...."

"No, that's affectation. I'm talking about instinct."

"Your terminology's as sloppy as ever. You call my instincts affectations and you call your instincts instincts."

"Alright, let's drop the theory. She has a lovely figure."

"Figure. You still use these quaint expressions."

"I'm adapting my vocabulary so you can understand what I'm saying."

"This must be a relic of that geometry theory you used to bore me with on quiet evenings, your great contribution to the science of sexual attraction. I put it all down to smell, personally."

"What smell do you go for?"

"Don't be stupid, Dermot. I'm talking about micro-odors, faint hormonal mistrals."

"I prefer something more explicit like Bal à Versailles."

They were cooler now and although the subject of Deborah had hardly been encroached upon they got to their feet and jogged back to the place where the bag with the soup and their clothes and their bus fare had once been. In retrospect the theft was inevitable—the park was a natural forum for misdemeanors of all kinds, from arson to self-exposure. They walked and ran home. Gary tried to beg for the fare home but the coins came slowly and tainted with abusive reluctance, a response which cheered him up no end since that was exactly how he would have reacted.

"Hello, can I speak to Dorothy please?"
"Is that Gary?"
"Yes it's Gary. That's Dorothy's mother, isn't it."
"No, it's Dorothy."
"Sorry Dorothy, it's a bad line."
"It's a good line. I obviously sound like my mother."
"I've apologized once."
"Do you know how old my mother is? *Do you know?*"
"Dorothy, why don't you shut up and come over to-night?"
"You're so *hurtful.*"
"Oh fuck off."

He put the phone down and wandered back to the kitchen. Boredom had him by the throat. Dermot had gone out and left him to the peace and darkness. Sunday evening, the saddest time.

Deborah was not upstairs, he had checked. He was checking regularly now, every fifteen minutes, in case she came in quietly under cover of noises in the street. The phone lay on its cradle in the hall but speaking to Dorothy had soured it for him. How dare she not ring back. Her return calls were one of the constants in their relationship, one of her devotional reflexes. Perhaps the wheel was turning; a woman can only take so much indifference before she starts to mimic her man and work his ploys better than he ever did. On the other hand Gary hated this Man and Woman business, it reminded him of men sitting in pubs giving birth painfully to generalizations they had half-heard on television. He read no novels and he had no time for abstractions, although he was partial to knowledge, which was an abstraction of a kind. He had no television because it made you stupid but he had a radio and knew all the wavelengths and all the voices. That was where most of his knowledge came from, the radio (which he had called the *wireless*

34

until recently when he realized the smart people were calling it the wireless again. Now he called it the *radio*). It was astonishing how much you could learn from the radio—if you listened to it long enough everything passed your way. Sport, drama, good news. Sometimes he kept it on at work, very low, like a real addict on intravenous sound. But that evening listening would have got on his nerves. He was irritated already listening to the ticking of his own brain. (They had these new telephones which had a button you could press to stop calls coming through; Gary was thinking of getting one for his head.)

He went back to the hall.

"Hello?"

"Hello Dorothy, I'm sorry I spoke to you like that."

"Wait a moment I'll get my daughter."

While he waited Gary cleaned his nails on the corner of the pink telephone directory.

"I'm sorry I spoke to you like that, Dorothy."

"She says she won't speak to you."

"Is there any particular reason?"

Gary could hear them debating this. Dorothy's mother was a fastidious intermediary; she wanted the reasons to make sense before she passed them on. He felt their mutual agitation down the wire.

"Gary?"

"Dorothy. I'm having trouble getting past your receptionist."

"I don't want to speak to you."

"I'm sorry about my harsh words, Dorothy." He was sorry.

"It's too late."

"Alright I'll call you in the morning."

"No it will be too late then."

Gary massaged his beard and then finished cleaning his nails on the corner of the pale blue telephone directory.

"Can I just recap for a moment, Dorothy. You don't want

to speak to me now and in the morning I'll be too late to be sorry. Is that a fair summary?" He heard her heavy sigh buffet the receiver at the other end.

"When was the last time you paid me a compliment, Gary?" she asked reasonably.

"It's never easy, is it, to pay people compliments."

"Never."

"No, it's never easy."

"You've never paid me a compliment. Never."

The conversation was going badly. It was shot through with pauses and riddled with chocks of silence.

"Not even at the beginning?" Gary was scouring his memory.

"No."

"Asking you out was a compliment."

"You only did it for the sex."

"That was probably the reason you accepted."

"Anyway I've met another man."

Gary bit his lip and chose between anger and ridicule. For a moment anger felt sweeter but ridicule was his natural medium. It was his crutch when he faltered.

"You've been hanging out in blind bars again, haven't you."

"Shut up."

"What do you expect me to say?—Did he go to a good school? Does he take his socks off last, the way women hate?" His voice was wavering and weakening from the realization that he was about to know misery. He had expected her to take him as he was but she had decided, finally, to take somebody else the way *he* was.

"We'd been going out together so rarely," she said evenly.

"Who?"

"You and me. Sometimes the phone didn't ring for days."

"You could have phoned me."

"You told me not to."

"I meant not all the time."

"It's too late now. I told him we'd split up."

"Ah well, if you've told him."

"You're not upset, are you Gary?"

"Actually I'm seeing another woman, Dorothy. I had intended to mention it." He didn't want to be so cheap. The words had escaped.

"What's her name?" Her lips sounded pursed.

"Deborah."

"What's she like?"

"Deborah? She's a lovely girl."

5th

The music on the radio was classical but not Dermot and Gary's idea of the best of the genre—they had in mind gale force violins or a cascading harp but the radio played bedlam scored for angry voice and maracas, or so it sounded.

"This always happens when I want something soothing like Bach or Beethoven or, what's the other B?" Gary asked.

"Bacharach."

"Brahms. And when I fancy some droopy French preludes they slap on a big band or this. I mean, listen to it. It's not doing any of the country any good."

"They have an incredible number of music hours to fill. Some of the stuff they put out is bound to have rough edges."

"But this is peak time. I won't tolerate rough edges. What's she singing about anyway?"

"I don't know. It sounds like German."

"German," Gary spat. Then he paused, winded. "God I'm in a bad mood."

Dermot put breakfast on the table. He had bought it the day before at the all-hours corner shop five corners away and it had cost him an arm and a leg. They had tried to charge him for a leg and two arms, it was that bad. Gary just sat there hunched, twisting his index finger in and out of his beard, irritating Dermot.

"I've split up with Dorothy, you know. We had a chat yesterday evening and decided we'd had enough."

"Well, it never really got off the ground, did it."

"Compared to some of your squalid little affairs, Dermot, we were in orbit."

"I was trying to be sympathetic."

"Anyway I explained what I felt and I must say she was quite frank."

"You're not upset are you, Gary?" She'd got rid of him, you didn't have to be clairvoyant. Gary had a low opinion of himself and Dermot often caught him tarting up the facts. Dermot never did that with his friends, though he might lie with strangers.

"Upset? No. You know how it was, there was a lot of convenience about it. I want to clear the deck for a new relationship."

"It was her idea, wasn't it." Dermot had had enough of this stupid talk. He sipped his grapefruit juice, looking over the glass at his friend's face. "You can be honest with me."

"I don't deny she suggested it."

"What did she say exactly?"

"That I never rang her up. She suspected I was seeing another woman."

Dermot didn't believe him. With a finger he idly spun his knife on the table, sighed and looked up.

"Gary, why don't you try being pleasant to the next one?"

Gary had had no other girlfriends while living with Dermot. Dorothy had been his only woman in that time. He had never brought to their flat after closing time a girl whose name he didn't know, giggling drunkenly and carrying one of her shoes. He had never returned home the following morning with shaky legs worrying about a toothbrush he had shared with a woman he met on a night bus. He had, in other words, led a perfectly normal life.

"But who are you to criticize?" he asked in a borrowed voice full of mildness.

"I don't want to sound harsh."

"So try something else," he said, his tone heating up.

"But it seems to me that you—"

"Are you going to go ahead and sound harsh or have you found some alternative?"

Dermot leaned back in his chair. "Would I be right in saying that you're awkward with women?"

"Look, I'm not doing this without a red velvet couch to lie on."

"You're very defensive."

"What am I supposed to do—take lessons from you in womencraft? Okay, so you're the only man on our block to hide his socks at the back of his condom drawer. I'm impressed. I'm amazed. What's your star sign? What's your favorite color? Can I have your phone number?"

One reason Gary was reticent with women was that he hated to be embarrassed. Without meaning to, necessarily, the women in his life had always located the nubs of his embarrassment. A reasonable mother, if she found a pornographic magazine under her young son's pillow, would say nothing; his own mother frogmarched him down to the newsagent and staged a scene, holding open a hideously fleshy gatefold in the middle of the shop, shouting and turning this way and that on her angry heel while Gary and the man behind the counter looked at the floor. An early girlfriend of Gary's once told a pubful of his friends that she had twice fallen asleep as he administered foreplay—*like a St. Bernard,* she had said, *the same wet lips and nose but without the brandy.* The thought of these paralyzing moments and others made him wary of meshing with the opposite sex without a lot of thought. Men were aware of the awkwardness of being a man and didn't show each other up, or only did so after much heartache.

How cruel would Deborah be?

Gary didn't have to work on Monday so Dermot went to work on his own. It was raining and the windows of the bus were steamed up. He kept his own section of window clear by rubbing it with his forearm to keep his eye on the static purlieus of

London, sleazy though they looked in the rheumatic autumn air.

He had been drinking the night before, on his own, and his tongue was a furry lizard. It was a habit of his to go into a pub, sit at the bar and wait for something to happen. Sometimes, to stretch his legs, he went out and sat at a table, took the paperback out of his pocket and read it while he waited. The chances were that nothing would happen, those were the chances, but once in a while he got drunk enough to talk to someone, probably a woman, or they got drunk enough to talk to him. He had only been behaving in this manner for about a year but it seemed like he'd been doing it forever.

The short walk to the department store was all hazards— umbrellas with eye-catching ribs made Dermot anxious and so did two beggars with their beseeching gaze and outstretched arms.

"Penny for the guy, mate."

"Call that a guy?" he stopped to say.

"Of course it's a fucking guy."

"It's a few plastic bags badly tied together."

"Use your imagination."

"And you imagine I've just given you a quid." They were about twelve years old and already seven feet tall. "And I bet you stole the pram."

"Yeah, we stole the pram."

At work Dermot was assigned to shifting. His suit, the only one of its kind, gathered the dust which slid from the boxed waffle irons and yogurt makers. He had to admit there was poetry in this business, the seamless flow of goods from warehouse to theirhouse. Dermot was modest about his own part in the process. (All he knew was he had done more aimless jobs before. Once he spent the day filing forms—he poured all his love into that work, teasing even the McCormacks from the McCormicks, the Deans from the DeAths—and was then told to put them through the shredder.) One great sadness was that the goods went to the wrong people, to the loose, careless, ungrateful money. The purchasers were more often defective than the goods—they were an unmatched pair or looked like they had fallen off the shelf, their fall only broken by a plastic mattress of credit cards. Dermot liked the older ladies who had no money but liked to browse, spending an hour or two among the decanters. They wore thick coats and he was terrified they would smash three months' pension with a rash swing of their hem, but they had good positional sense. He had nothing against the customers with money except that they had lost their awe; Dermot was perpetually poor and when he bought something as simple as a toaster he became speechless with excitement. It was a grotesque enthusiasm, perhaps.

When he had finished arranging the yogurt makers into an irresistibly attractive formation Dermot stood around attracting questions.

"Excuse me, do you work here?"

"Yes, madam."

"Do you know what a runcible spoon is?"

"I'm afraid I've no idea."

"It's a three-pronged fork."

"Right. Thanks."

As he had been urged in Training, Dermot occasionally forced himself to assist the floundering customer.

"Sir, can I help?"

"No."

Or to volunteer information:

"Guaranteed for two years madam," he whispered into a dowager's wiry gray temple.

"But it's a broom. What could go wrong with a broom?"

"You'd be surprised. People are always bringing them back."

"I don't think I want one then."

"You're right. How about the Robovac? A shade noisier than a broom but it's a sexy little machine."

"What does it do?"

"I'm not really sure."

The unblinking truth. They loved that.

"Sir had fallen asleep."

"What?" The man was tugging his sleeve.

"It often happens, I'm afraid. We normally allow customers twenty minutes and then we rouse them gently."

"I'm dreadfully sorry." Gary got to his feet all groggy and saw that the afternoon light had certainly become twenty minutes older. As a measure of good faith he agreed to buy the sleep-inducing bed.

"It has an interior-sprung mattress."

"The springs are inside, are they? That's a good idea. How long will you take to deliver it?"

"About three weeks."

"Come off it, I can't wait that long." Gary had not signed for it but the cashier allowed himself to ghost a simper across his face, risking his commission. "Look. I sell stamps for a living—what would happen if I took three weeks to deliver them? You may well shrug your shoulders."

Eventually they promised to deliver it within a fortnight and he went to the bed linen department. He found some black sheets and, thinking that would look smart, bought two pairs and carried them home.

Dermot rushed home with Deborah in his head. He didn't want to meet her on the stairs because he had a plant for her. A cactus.

"Your mother phoned," Gary told him as he crossed the hall.

"What did she say?" Dermot was in a hurry and not sure what to wear.

"She kept calling you Duncan," he shouted through from the kitchen, "have you got a brother called Duncan?"

"I believe I have." Dermot's family was a large one. He had four brothers and two sisters and enough satellite relatives to start a small galaxy.

"I put her right, name-wise. She expects you home one of these weekends."

"She's always getting our names wrong."

"I'll say that for my parents, they always get my name okay."

"It's hardly the same if you're an only child. And your father's called Gary." Dermot was breathless from pulling off his suit, changing his socks and crawling into a cupboard to get his boots. They smelt of the spring, when he last had them on.

"Was that a plant I saw in your hand?"

"Yes, it's a cactus for Deborah." There was a silence and Dermot stopped pulling on his trousers in case he missed a sigh or a snort or an expletive from the kitchen. "Go on, put me through it. Tell me she's out of my class."

Heavily, he replied, "She's out of your class."

"I've asked her out tonight."

"And she said Yes, as long as you give me a plant."

"Something like that." He resumed his dressing, hesitating a while over the shirt and wondering if he had time to sew on some buttons or scratch off some stains.

Dermot knew that Gary didn't like this arrangement. So awkward, jealousy.

Upstairs Deborah took the cactus and invited him into her room, which was warm and alive with personal possessions not close enough to examine properly, photographs and intimabilia. There were yellow knickers hanging out of a drawer and she tucked them in with a slick whirl of her arm.

Dermot knew he spoke ridiculously when he was nervous so he was chary about speaking at all.

"When do the fireworks begin?" she asked at length as she put one arm in her coat. Dermot leapt up to assist her in placing the other arm.

"I forgot to check. I've made an educated guess at eight o'clock."

They left Deborah's attic bedsit with its views over back gardens with sheds, grass rectangles and cloudy greenhouses, and went downstairs in their coats and gloves. As he passed his own door Dermot diplomatically lightened his tread but Deborah seemed if anything to click her heels emphatically on the uncarpeted boards.

He didn't want to upset Gary because they had a rapport, something to do with living together for the past two years. In one respect he was glad Gary was interested in Deborah, his girl—Gary needed more interests.

"I'm sorry I interrupted you at work," he said as they walked in light rain to the bus stop. "How long have you been working there?"

"Three days. The people there seem easy to get on with. They've tolerated my moods so far."

"You don't strike me as being moody." Dermot was bad on character, a lazy observer most of the time. He had sat through the dinner they had together ignoring her personality, watching her steady eyes and her lips. She didn't sparkle and her words were dry. If he had to describe her now he would call her inward-looking, calculating. But, really, he was no good at descriptions.

"Why did you ask me out?" she suddenly asked and looked at him, one cheek and ear lit by the tangerine streetlights.

"To see the fireworks."

"You could have seen them on your own."

"I like you. You're my neighbor."

"I suppose you want to sleep with me after the fireworks."

This was unorthodox, this was unusual, or simply childish.

"Is that alright with you?"

"It's alright you wanting."

She reproduced her inward smile. Dermot was edgy now and expected her to do something unexpected. She seemed to want to drop the subject, however, from the way she was looking straight ahead with an unexpression on her face.

"Statistically, I gather, couples normally go to bed on their third date," Dermot decided to say, not wanting to drop the subject at all, "but that's only an average. I would imagine the odd couple needs about thirty dates and drags the average up. Perhaps you're right, it's best to get it out in the open."

"Settle on a time-scale, you mean." Now Dermot could tell she was being cynical. It was the kind of thing Gary would say. "Let's not be proud, let's stick to the national average. Fireworks, cinema, atmospheric dinner, and then sex."

"Okay."

"No."

They stood quietly at the bus stop. Dermot told her that he seemed to spend his whole life waiting for or sitting on buses and the words tumbled out in billows of white vapor because it was cold. Car headlights illuminated a miasma of workmanlike drizzle. The bus shelter kept them dry in the dark but black streams of water gathered at their feet. Dermot loved the summer, he thought autumn was a disgrace. He remembered standing at the same bus stop in July, happy in shirt and shorts and hoping this year he would be able to get away to the heat, like the birds. He wanted the seasons torn up and air conditioning put in.

This year nobody had lit the bonfire a day early but most of the fireworks had gone off before Dermot's educated guess because, apparently, children tired easily and early and by eight o'clock they were lethally irritable. The bonfire remained and they stood close to the heat. Pieces of household furniture caught his eye, the skeleton of an armchair and the door of a wardrobe, hanging on against the flames. Deborah looked impassively into the burning heart of the fire as around them parents led their sons and daughters away into the ring of darkness. The incandescence held Dermot and Deborah, silent and staring, for a full half-hour and then they went for a drink.

Dermot had developed simple equations involving personality and the alcohol a person chose, but Deborah had orange juice.

The problem of sex and courtship, was it such a problem? It seemed that way. What they actually talked about was the best way to remove red wine stains from pale carpets at parties. Dermot advocated moving an item of furniture, anything but a glass-topped table, over the mess. Soon he threw this conversation on the fire and started again.

"Tell me about Mike."

"Who's Mike?"

"Gary said you lived with a man called Mike. I hope he hasn't been lying to me."

"No, I was with him for about a year. We were very cruel to each other."

"Whose fault was it?"

"His."

"Why did you stay?"

"He had a nice bottom. I didn't ask myself questions about what I was doing. He didn't ask questions either."

"I'm afraid I do. I'm incredibly considerate."

Dermot was impressed with the change that had come over her. She was beginning to criticize him, dissent was turning out to be her natural dialect, as it was Gary's and as it was his, sometimes. They would have good arguments together. Arguments were the way people conducted their business nowadays, people were too prosaic to make lyrical speeches and too rowdy to connive in easy agreements.

"I'll tell you what he was," she volunteered in her clear but skeptical voice.

"Go on."

"He was rich and he spent money on me."

"You had no qualms about taking money off him?"

"It was blood money. I told him quite clearly that the only reason I stayed with him was his money."

"You didn't mention his bottom?"

"Only in passing."

Dermot put his hands through his light brown hair, one set of fingers cold on his ear from clutching the pint glass, and asked a serious question. "You think money's important, do you? You see, I haven't got any."

"To be honest, Dermot, I can't see us getting very far without it. I've had poor boyfriends before."

"How bad was it?"

"It varied."

"But what happened to traditional criteria, like decency and sexual performance?"

"I take them all into account. I suppose your own preconditions all center around moral beauty. From the look in your eyes the whole time, and the way they follow my body around, I wouldn't imagine you were too bothered with decency. I've been messed around by men enough to appreciate that the percentage of their disposable income that they spend on me can be as good a guide to their love as any."

"If you're talking about percentages I agree with you. You realize that in my case even half my pay packet wouldn't keep you in orange juice. Mind you, I'm willing to pool my debts."

6 th

"Nice weekend, Gary?"

"No George."

"The wife and I went down to Rugby."

"I always say up."

"How do you mean?"

"I always say I went *up* to Rugby."

"Do you go a lot, then, Gary? You ought to visit my sister."

"No, I'm talking about prepositions. I say down to Croydon but up to Rugby."

"Why's that then?"

"I suppose it's because it looks up on the map when you're driving along and holding it in your hand." It was a quiet day and their conversation was dilatory.

"Of course problems arise when you want to go to Windsor."

"I know. All those tourists under your feet."

"No, I mean do you say up or down to Windsor?"

"Across."

Gary was sifting through some Victorian letters. The sepia copperplate had reactivated his sense of history and he had unfolded the wrapper and started to read the contents.

"Here George, listen to this old letter. 'Since your visit I have scarce had time to collect my thoughts. My pulse quickens when I think of your hands in my summerhouse and

51

the magnitude of your desiring. My thighs'—it becomes indistinct here."

"Does it really say that?"

"No. I can't read the handwriting on these things. Too many loops."

Gary only sold British stamps and was thinking of even greater specialization. Dermot had suggested he just sell blue ones. The profession had lost most of its fascination by now and Gary was sometimes ashamed to admit what he did for a living. He had to deal in particular with schoolboys and spiky sexagenarians who spent their retirements poring over catalogs (Gary sometimes thought stamp collecting was the perfect metaphor for the pointlessness of human existence. He hadn't told George).

"So what was wrong with your weekend then, Gary?"

"Little things. I lost some clothes. Dermot's getting on my nerves."

"Isn't it time you bought a place of your own? You must have a heap of money saved up."

"It's all tied up in these bloody stamps. Besides what would Dermot do?"

"You sound like a right poof sometimes, Gary."

Gary was lying. He had a heap of liquid money and was happy watching it accumulate. If he had to be honest he was waiting for one of his rich remaining grandparents to die, leaving what one had called "a tidy sum" and the other "a small something for you to start a family with" as if a family was a dry-cleaning business. Then he would sell all his stamps, buy a house and plan a radical new future. Alternatively, he would do none of these things.

He had been lying about Dermot, too. Although he cared a little about his friend, he did not now care a lot. They were going to fall out over that girl because Dermot had known how keen he had been, he must have done, but still Dermot had gone ahead and taken her to the fireworks. *He* wanted to take her to the fireworks. He *adored* fireworks. The split with Dorothy had been a poke in the eye and Dermot had manhandled his sickly pride. Deborah was a different matter. He would stalk her and put Dermot in the shade (though that was incidental).

"Guess what I bought yesterday, George," he called through the partition in his brown voice.

"A hat?"

"No."

"A chair?"

"No."

"Can I stop guessing now?"

"Oh come on, it passes the time."

"Television?"

"No."

"Parrot?"

"No. Now you're just guessing."

"Bicycle?"

"No."

"Dishwasher?"

"No."

"Crate of champagne?"

"No."

"A hat?"

"You already said hat."

"Bicycle?"

"You already said bicycle."

"Was it a bicycle?"

"No."

"Dinner service, roller skates?"

"One at a time. It lasts longer."

"Dinner service?"

"No. Nor roller skates."

"Newspaper?"

"No."

"Tell me."

"What's the hurry? We've got the rest of our lives."

"Hat?"

"Close enough. A double bed, very expensive."

"What happened to your old one?"

"Worn out."

"All that bouncing around, eh? You young people."

"That's the way we are, George. We young people need to bounce around a great deal."

"The sexual revolution."

"Don't blame me, George."

Gary saw out the morning in this sauntering fashion and then heaved the shutter shut. Usually he stayed at his post with a cup of coffee and a gross of sandwiches in order to mop up some of the money that was out and about during lunch hours as a rule, but today he strolled out into the cold midday and made his way toward Deborah. She was half a mile west across town, unless he'd misheard her fleeting reference to the wholefood café where she said she worked (Or was the *wholefood* his own invention? He occasionally embellished). But somewhere along the route he lost his nerve and turned into a restaurant to eat alone. Not knowing what to say to her, he realized, could have left him in the dirt; you really need to know what you are going to tell a person, unless spontaneity does something for you or for the quality of your conversation. So he sat at his table for two and ordered a small pizza, because he was dieting, slimming for Deborah. He denied himself a side whack of calories and turned his head from the carbohydrate trolley. He also made his mind up to leave something on the side of his plate but through force of habit he forgot to leave anything there apart from his knife and fork, prettily arranged at twenty-five past five.

Gary hadn't spoken to Dermot but he'd made sure Dermot had slept in his own bedroom. They hadn't met at breakfast and that was rare, so rare that he had poured two cups of tea instead of one, like a grieving widower. An unpleasant image came to Gary of Dermot's fingers slipping under the forgiving waistband of her tracksuit and, worse, of her acquiescence, which revealed itself in a shift in her breathing from soft and regular to heavy and spasmodic. He almost changed his mind and went to see Deborah, to talk to her about this imaginary behavior of hers, but instead he went back to his stall and prepared some phrases that she might like to hear that evening.

The afternoon went as slowly as the morning and the dusk came down early at about half past three. All the lights in the arcade were switched on and the dealers watched each other and did not say a word.

Gary's progress home was slower than ever on the bus, it would have been quicker to walk, so he got off and tried to catch the underground. Unfortunately somebody was *under a train* further up the line and it would have been quicker to walk or go by bus. He waited on the crowded platform and wondered what it was like to commit yourself to jumping *under a train;* did you, let's think, buy the cheapest ticket or did you—insanely—buy a return to a far outpost, Ongar? Did you remember to jump off (first stop on the Mystery Tour) at the correct end of the platform, where the train was going at a murderous speed? Were you so committed to this act that you did not allow yourself hope of reprieve because, for example, *somebody else* had jumped under a train further up the line, thereby disrupting services? He once heard someone bitterly complaining that it was an antisocial form of suicide (and it was, it was) and Gary was ashamed of the man's bitterness— didn't he understand anything about despair, that it is never sociable?

When Gary got home he went straight up to Deborah's room and knocked on the door.

"Come in."

He stepped into the room, saying nothing.

"How are you?" she said and went on stirring a saucepan.

"Fine. Are you settling in all right?"

"You asked me that the last time."

"I thought it was a continual process. You may have done it well at first, no problems, and then, bang!, two really rough days of settling in."

"No."

"Good."

He walked over to the window, scratching his beard, and

looked out. "Just look into all those sitting rooms. It always reminds me of seeing inside someone's mouth when they yawn in public. Private places." This felt too fey. He turned back and watched Deborah stirring in silence on her single burner. "Do you want to borrow anything?"

"I don't think so."

"Coffee, string?"

"Not even string."

"What are you doing this evening?"

"Going out with an old friend."

"What do you do when you go out?"

"It depends. What do you do?"

"I like to stay at home. I tend to listen to the radio and play cards."

"Isn't that lonely?"

"I find it relaxing. You can cheat without your opponent asking you to step outside."

This was a tame picture he was painting, the portrait of a masturbator with gray skin and bedsocks. Well so be it. He would make his gray existence a thing of beauty.

"Why do people want to go out all the time? I think it's because they're too scared to listen to their heartbeats and sit in silence with their souls."

"I thought you said you had the radio on."

He ignored her sudden asperity. It might disappear as it had come. "Thinking distinguishes us from animals and you can't think if you're dancing or watching a film." He had to agree there were holes in his argument you could push a tree through, but he went on. "And if you tell me the mind needs stimulation from human contact, I have to say I get all the human contact I need during the day. By the way, what are you doing tomorrow evening?"

"Is this a factual inquiry or an invitation to spend an evening with you listening to the World Service?"

"It's an invitation to go somewhere, maybe to a restaurant." The line came out easily; Gary traced his restfulness to the hypnotic rhythm of her hand on the wooden spoon and the ripples this sent out to the corners of her body. His mind went back (it was in permanent reverse) to his geography teacher, a siren whose shoulders and hips jigged in sympathy when she drew Scotland's ragged coastline in thick chalk on the board, or wrote wobble words like *Mississippi* and *Wagga Wagga*. Sexual inklings come in many forms and Gary's came in the second form.

Her arm slowed for a moment and then accelerated again.

"Is this some kind of competition between you and Dermot?"

"No. I keep my affections to myself."

"Difficult to believe. Come on, tell me the rules. Am I the only prize or is there a cash bet on the side?"

"I swear to you." He drew breath. "Dermot's like a rat up a drainpipe. He forages for sex the whole time. I don't want to condemn him out of hand because it's just another way of living a life but, really, he's just out to give himself a good time." Put like that, he realized, she'd probably prefer Dermot. If he'd been her *he* would have preferred Dermot, no question.

"*I* like a good time," she actually said. Her stew seemed to be burning; it was giving off a sore smell.

"So come out with me tomorrow."

"Let me just say something. I've had a hard time recently with men and I've got little to be confident about in that line. If I go out with you even once I don't just want a good time, I want a *very* good time. I want surprises. I'll mess you about and not say thank you."

It was a speech. Gary was almost moved, although what she had to say had been chilling in its implications. A relationship based on surprises needed a special kind of stamina; she didn't want a partner, she wanted an impresario.

"Boo," he said loudly, to surprise her.

"That will do to start with." She turned off the gas and generated a disconcerting smile.

"I suppose you want to eat that on your own."

"No, I want to tell the time with it."

Gary wondered how long she could keep *that* up.

"Half past seven tomorrow, then," he said at the door.

"Eight o'clock," she answered and sat down to eat.

7th

There were noises on the stairs. On the landing, commotion.

"Gary, Dermot!" Geraldine shouted through the door and banged on it. "I need to talk to you."

Dermot was pulling up his trousers and Gary was lying in bed listening to his own heartbeat.

"Boys, boys!"

Dermot fastened the belt at leisure and walked to all that banging.

"Stop that percussion, Geraldine. I'm on my way." His voice was a rasp, from all that drinking the night before, and even he could see that his suit trousers and the luggage under his eyes were unsightly.

"It's Gerald," she said when the door was open.

"Don't play games, Geraldine. I can see it's you." It was cruel of him—she was not hiding her distress. If he had to guess, he would have said she'd been up all night or at least up as much of the night as it took to make her look that tired.

"No, it's Gerald."

"What's happened?"

"He's gone."

"What did you say?"

"I said he's gone."

"I mean what did you say to make him go?" Dermot said to himself *discretion,* think about what you're saying for once in your life. "Did you have an argument?"

"Not particularly."

"Has he left just now?"

"No, I haven't seen him since yesterday morning."

Dermot was leading this conversation but wanted to be led. What should he say now?"

"Tea?" he asked, sympathetically.

"Yes."

He went into the kitchen and put the kettle on. She hadn't followed him in so he went back to fetch her from the hall, where she still stood, overawed by events, in a quilted house-coat.

"I don't know what to do," she said in her spindly voice and sat down in the chair Gary liked to use.

"Let's proceed one step at a time. Did Gerald give any indication that he might be going away? Think carefully and then answer."

"No."

It wasn't as easy as it looked. Cross-examination was another skill he didn't have. He would have preferred something simple for his first case—an absconded pet, some casual burglary. Ideally, at this stage, Dermot would have poured himself three fingers of bourbon and called in Gary "Fat Boy" Strang, his sleeping partner. He poured two fingers of milk and made tea.

"Has he taken anything?"

"Not even a toothbrush."

"Have you called the police?"

"I'd rather not just yet. I'll call the gallery later."

"Gary told me you thought there might be another woman."

"Well he was getting back late all the time, always blaming the traffic and of course he traveled by tube. He knew it was a stupid joke but I thought maybe he was out drinking with the men from work." Her customary excess in the way she talked (her idiom was vocative—"Boys, boys!"—like a first Latin grammar) was missing.

"Perhaps that's what he was doing. A man often needs the company of other men, if only so he can talk about women undisturbed. Did he mention any special friends?"

"No."

"No lingering over certain names, no talking in his sleep?"

"I said no, no."

Dermot couldn't imagine another woman was involved. His money was on an accident of some kind or amnesia or madness. Dermot thought back to his own talks with Gerald and could only remember being affected by his resignation. Behind his gloomy eyes, Dermot guessed, more gloom. He liked his landlord and wished it was something as simple as another woman. To him the word *mistress* had a homely and traditional sound, it seemed like a word you could take home to your mother, or your wife.

"I really have to go now, Geraldine. I'll ring you in my lunch hour. I'm sure there's an explanation."

Gary walked in as he left and they sketched a greeting with their hands.

"I'm sorry, I missed that, Geraldine..." Dermot heard as he closed the door behind him. He went down the stairs, running his finger like a child along the flock fleurs-de-lis until it burned, and through the bold pink door. Gerald had repaired the front gate, which had swung off its hinges in a September gale. Gary wondered if this would turn out to be his last piece of maintenance. The front garden was in a state of neglect which detracted in a small way from the new, dreamy swing of the gate.

Dermot didn't want to be late for work so it made him all the more livid when he was at least three minutes late.

"Ten past nine." His supervisor.

"In fact I arrived at this store at three minutes past. There was a bottleneck on the staff staircase."

"You would have been late anyway." He was tapping his watch as if it was a barometer.

"And I'll tell you why. My landlady's husband has disappeared and I had to calm her down." Dermot expected his supervisor to crumble in his hands and force upon him a month of compassionate leave.

"I don't like my staff to exploit my sympathy."

"These were the facts. I thought her predicament was worth three minutes of the company's time."

"Ten minutes."

"However many minutes. Thirty."

Dermot was summoned to the personnel department at the end of the morning. He assumed they wanted to sack him for timekeeping, rather than offer him a seat on the board. They wanted to transfer him to the bookshop on the first floor. Apparently he had passed the right number of exams to cope with the bookish inquiries; there had been complaints that the existing staff were *unscholarly* and in some cases downright *incurious*. He spoke to a pleasant woman up there on the fifth floor.

"Will I be earning any more money now?"

"No dear."

"But I've moved up two floors."

"Look darling. We don't pay by altitude."

"It was just a thought I had."

Dermot didn't have many friends in the basement so he did not go down and kiss any cheeks. Since his first day at the shop, when he was as sociable as it was possible to be, Dermot had toned down his behavior. He took a book into the canteen and read it quietly. Before, he would have bothered one of the cosmetic operatives from the ground floor, who sat behind their makeup and nibbled at hamster-sized lunches, but he was faithful to Deborah now.

There was a problem over money. She was testing him, you didn't have to be a psychologist, and in order to pass the test he had to get hold of a lot of money and spend it on her. He had no money. In fact he had minus money—there was a hole where it used to be, called overdraft. Dermot had an arrangement with his bank manager whereby he, Dermot, gave money to the bank every quarter in order to buy their silence and dig even deeper into the hole. Sometimes Gary would bail him out, because Gary was Croesus-rich. There could be no more of that, it had to stop.

They led Dermot to the book department, where he was briefed on the theory and practice of selling.

"We like to think that selling books is different from selling cookers."

"You need to sell more books to make the same amount of money."

"That's what I mean."

"Pile them high and sell them before lunch."

"Exactly. I'm afraid that Personnel makes noises about catering to the individual's requirements."

"But what do they know about the realities of the marketplace?" Dermot could lock into conversations like this and it might take minutes for his interlocutor to wonder about his sincerity. In fact he was not being insincere, he had simply entered a fugue state and was not thinking at all.

"It's usually laziness anyway. The customer knows she won't find *A Tale of Two Cities* under 'Maps and Guides' but runs to the hard-pressed assistant to ask where it might possibly be."

"They say they've heard about a novel from a friend all about a man and a woman, the title starts with a P or an S, and they expect you to find it for them."

"Although of course we must take all reasonable measures. I don't want to see rudeness."

"I think the public deserves more than rudeness."

They went on in this rich vein of understanding and then Dermot was allowed to drift around in his new home getting the feel of the carpet.

At lunchtime he went to the phone rank on the fifth floor. He emptied his pockets and found plenty of change but none of it the right size.

"Excuse me have you got any ten-pence pieces?"

"I need all mine for the meter."

"Excuse me can you help me out with a ten-pence piece?"

"I have to call my mother."

"Do you have two ten-pences for a twenty?"

"Are three twos any good to you?"

63

"Have you got ten pence for the phone?"

"I never give change."

Finally he found what he was looking for at the bottom of a young woman's handbag which, she casually revealed, also contained a tin of cocktail sausages.

"Hello Geraldine."

"Who's that?"

"Dermot. Any news?"

"He's disappeared. He hasn't turned up for work." She sounded calm, hysterically calm.

"Have you called the police?"

"No."

"Why not?"

"I'm afraid of what they might say."

"It's something you've got to do Geraldine. What did they say at the gallery?"

"They were cross at first because it left the Titians vulnerable, they said, but I'm afraid I started to cry and the man said he understood."

"That's something."

"This is awful."

"I have to go now, Geraldine." It was like visiting a patient in hospital. There was a need for the same assuring tone. "Don't forget to call the police and make sure you have some lunch."

He felt like a surrogate son and indeed he was. She had never had children "because of poor Gerald's sperm count." From the pity and derision in her voice it must have been only two or three.

With the other coin he got through to the bank.

"I'd like to speak to Mr. Swallow please."

"I'm sorry, he's at lunch."

"That's the only time I can ring, you see. During my lunch hour. As one door opens, another closes."

"Perhaps you could pop your inquiry in the post. What is it regarding?"

"A rather personal matter. It's regarding money."

"Ah. A money matter."

"Could I see him tomorrow do you think?"

"Not in his lunch hour I wouldn't have thought. He eats at home with his wife."

"You're right, I wouldn't feel comfortable. Actually tomorrow's my day off so I could come in the morning."

"I'll just check if he's free." Dermot heard the rustle of important financial documents and in the background a very slow typist was leaving islands of silence between each character.

"I expect he's a busy man," he murmured, in case she thought he'd gone away. Dermot was not actually interested in how busy he was.

"Very busy." She kept on flicking and in the background the typist had fallen asleep at the keys. "When would you like to come?" she asked.

"Half past nine."

"Fine, I'll pencil you in Mr.?"

"Thank you."

"Mr.?"

"Bye-bye then."

"What's your *name?*"

"Dermot Povey."

"How do you spell it?"

"The normal way. Like poverty, without the R or the T." He was pleased with that. It hadn't been planned.

Gary had spent a difficult afternoon organizing surprises. Naturally, he had discussed the problem with George.

"When I was courting my wife" (Gary loved to hear old words like *courting*), "I used to surprise her with flowers."

"How did you do that, George?"

"What do you mean? I *bought* them for her, that's how I surprised her with them."

"Didn't it stop being a surprise after a while?"

"She never said so."

"The trouble is, a modern girl expects more. I think if I

wanted to surprise Deborah with flowers I'd have to juggle with them."

"Can you juggle?"

"Look, it wasn't a serious suggestion. It was an example of our blunted appetites."

"What about chocolates? During rationing after the war you could buy a girl's heart with a box of soft centers."

"But if you had big money then what would you have done?"

"I'd have bought Marjorie a fox. She always wanted one of the foxes with the head and the feet left on that you wrap around your neck."

"I can't see Deborah wanting one of those either."

"It's funny how tastes change. One minute it's fox stoles, the other it's something else. What is it now?"

"That's what I need to know."

"I'm afraid I've been no help."

Gary shut his shop early again. (It was not the first time that week that his routine had been twisted out of shape. His life was becoming floppy and indistinct. Leaving half an hour early, Gary felt personal anarchy in his veins.) He walked to a clutch of shops and stared purposefully through the first window. A building society. As he moved to the next window, his furled umbrella swung from his forearm. There were surprises to be had in chemist shops but today he was not tempted. Next door was a florist and Gary went in and bought the largest cactus there was, a towering succulent with harsh green branches that were not easy to wrap. The florist's hands darted back and forth to her spinning wheel of tape and Gary watched to see if she would prick her finger on the plant's cruel spines. She did not, but he did as he eased himself into a taxi. He had never taken a taxi home from work before; even when he had cash in four figures stuffed in open-ended manila and nesting against his ribs Gary used public transport. On other occasions he would have enjoyed the challenge of taking a large cactus on the underground at prime time, when so many people least expected it. But tonight he already had challenges.

He sat back in the seat and quietly observed the nonsmoking rule and the back of the driver's head. The sliding window was open and the back of the head spoke. "Shopping?"

"Yes. I always shop for essentials on Wednesday nights."

"What have you got there?"

"Antlers."

Gary paid from a fold of notes and tipped, by his hasty computations, seventeen, eighteen percent?

There was a light behind Geraldine's curtains and Gary fought his conscience and won. He would not be popping in to chat, nor did he often. You could say he had the measure of his conscience.

He tripped at the bottom of the stairs, however, and brought his landlady to the door inadvertently.

"I think I've broken a leaf off," he said, and palpated the paper to check for damage. Geraldine looked worse than in the morning—it was true that grief made you smaller; worry made your shoulders hunch and your cheeks suck against your teeth. He had assumed Gerald would have returned by now trailing an elaborate excuse.

"I rang the police," she explained in her new low register. "Nobody's been brought in."

"Is anybody looking after you?" he asked.

"Gwen's here."

"Shall I send her away and find someone more congenial?"

"What do you mean?"

"I'm saying I know how depressing Gwen can be on her bad days."

"No. She's making me coffee."

"Is there anything you'd like me to do?"

"I can't think."

"You've contacted all his relatives and been through his pockets for clues?"

"Yes. Gwen thinks something awful's happened to him."

"I imagined that would be her diagnosis." He really should send her home.

"There is one thing you could do."

"What's that?"

"Go round and see if he's in a pub somewhere."

"Where somewhere? Where would I start?"

"I thought we could start with London."

"Have you any idea how many pubs there *are* in London? Geraldine, there are more pubs than people, that's how many. And you said he didn't drink."

"He didn't normally, but disappearing isn't normal."

Geraldine's face quickly lost its look of colorless marble and began to fold and fault and corrugate, spitting out chipped words that were lost in tears. Gary had seen her cry before but somehow it always came as a surprise because in the past he had associated weeping with men. When men cried it got reported. At the two funerals he had attended the men wept, not the women. In his own home only his father used to cry (but he no longer bothered); if his mother had any sadness she could not channel into words, she would keep it to herself and pay it out gradually. This time Gary was more than surprised, he was appalled. For the second time within a week he held Geraldine to his chest and let her quake there for a minute while the violence drained from her face.

"All you can do is wait," he told her. She went inside and the closing of the door guillotined her whimpers.

Gary picked up his cactus, impaled his fingers.

Upstairs he ran a bath. He was a fastidious and regular bather, soaping away the sins of the world with his thick fingers. His routine was as fixed as the constellations from the turn of the first tap to the reshelving of his Mr. Men shampoo. The only variable was the temperature of the water, which he had never been able to judge. Tonight he ran it too hot and came out molten.

"Can I come in?" he said through the yawning door.

"Of course."

"You're sure that's not too conventional a start to the evening?"

"Don't be stupid." She didn't look ready to go out and her

68

mood looked unforgiving. Gary was wearing a suit with sharp creases. Deborah was wearing her old tracksuit, no creases.

"I've come too smart, haven't I."

She moved busily about the room. "It depends. Not if we're going to a wedding. What's this?"

"A plant."

"Didn't anybody ever tell you two boys that you don't give cacti to a lady." As Gary had hoped, she put the pot next to Dermot's dwarfish offering.

"No, nobody ever told me that." Was this true? "Are there any other rules I should know about?"

"As far as I know that's the only one."

He went up to her and tried to kiss her on the cheek, there being no other rules. She responded by moving back two steps to the stove and picking up the saucepan. Her arm went back behind her shoulder and was poised to bury the saucepan in Gary's temple when there was an indeterminate noise on the stairs and then a cantankerous dialogue at the door followed by a double entrance. Dermot and another. The other was angry, like Dermot.

"Who are these bastards?"

Deborah stepped forward, the best of hostesses.

"Dermot, Gary, this is Mike. You'll find Mike's manners leave a lot to be desired. In fact, they're not manners at all."

There was a hiatus while they each registered their alarm. Mike was as tall as Gary, that is to say tall but he carried his weight across his chest. Gary rested his on his trouser belt. Deborah's ex-lover was a triangle with broad shoulders tapering to his feet, whereas Gary had the shape of a Russian doll.

At first Gary thought Deborah was enjoying herself but he seemed to have got that wrong. She was clenching and unclenching her fists and her teeth were clamped furiously together.

"I asked who are these bastards," he repeated and thrust his hands into the pockets of his distressed leather jacket.

"Who are you, bastard?" Dermot said, thinking that would bring the man over to his side breathing casual violence.

Instead he went to Deborah and put an arm around her shoulder. He had two feet of arm to spare. On two of his fingers unreasonable signet rings crouched.

"I don't like this man calling me a bastard, Dermot," Gary said levelly.

"I know what you mean, Gary. It's a worrying development."

"What did we do to the last one that did that, Dermot?"

"We were quite tetchy with him."

"Tetchy. Testy."

Mike shifted his weight from one foot to the other and performed a bullying smile. Deborah tried to walk away but he held her shoulder.

"Comedians."

Once again Gary felt he was dressed badly for the occasion. If he got into a fight he would cut his legs on his trouser creases.

"You know what I'm thinking, Dermot?"

"Are you thinking like me that this streak of shit's trousers are too tight for his own safety?"

"I don't deny that's been worrying me, Dermot. But I'll tell you what I was mainly thinking. Why has he got his arm round this person, round our Deborah?"

"I'm glad you brought that up, Gary."

It would have been dangerous to pursue this line of argument. Deborah's position needed to be clarified. She may have invited him over. She may still love him. Two minutes ago she'd had a saucepan cocked over Gary's head and all he'd wanted to do was surprise her.

Mike had lost all of his smile and his hand was dangling over Deborah's right breast.

"Mike, I want you to leave. How did you find my address?"

"One of your friends let it slip. Send your minders away, I want to talk to you."

She sighed. It must have been embarrassing for her. "I have nothing to say to you."

70

He said, "Deborah and I lived together. She's in love with me really. I don't think she wants to say it in front of you."

"It looks like she loves you. That must be why she's so keen to talk to you."

"And that would account for her tongue being in your mouth, and her general enthusiasm."

Deborah freed herself finally and danced to the door. She held it open. "I don't want to see you again, Mike."

He must have been pleased with his visit because he left quietly with a smirk frozen into his face.

8 th

Dermot needed this day off. He got up late to show how much he needed it.

Gary had long gone and the kitchen showed no sign that he had ever been there. Dermot didn't cover his traces so fussily—he liked people to know exactly where he had been and what he'd been doing.

Gary should have had a happy breakfast, having taken Deborah out. He shouldn't have done it if it wasn't going to make him happy.

After seeing Mike off they had all three sat in front of the fire and watched the single orange bar. Nobody could bear to make too much of the fact that a man had pushed his way through two doors and said harsh things. Deborah hadn't felt the need to explain or apologize, or perhaps she felt the need but had still gone ahead and not done either. Dermot had his doubts about people who didn't apologize. They converted all their guilty energy into justifying themselves either insidiously or in speeches. On the other hand she hadn't done anything wrong apart from getting involved with a man who probably broke heads for a living. It happens. If Deborah's trade was lifting wallets it would not have kept Dermot from having her round, though he might screw down his furniture. But Dermot claimed that when he was growing up people accounted for their actions, explaining what they were going to do and why, what they had done and why, what their friends had done and why. In a family his size if he put his coat on to go out he had to explain three or four times where he was going before they let him reach the front door. There was a different system now.

"Good morning. I've come to see the manager."

"Name?"

"Swallow."

"I should think you'll get on with him then. *His* name's Swallow too."

"I know. *My* name's not Swallow."

Their conversation had unraveled. It lay on the counter between them.

"Perhaps I should come in again and *you* play the customer this time," he said, and smiled. She looked at him as if he wasn't there.

"Name?"

"Povey."

"You're down for nine thirty."

"I'm very very sorry."

"It's eleven seventeen."

"Yes, I should have rung to explain I'd be late."

"Please take a seat."

He considered the question of Gary while he watched money slip from one side to the other of the bulletproof glass. It seemed that Deborah might be having difficulty in distinguishing between the two of them. Gary, remember, was the taller, bearded man. Pay attention. Just because they shared a flat and the same age, she didn't have to *treat* them the same. He, remember, was lithe and fair with no beard and had peeled away all artifice on the way home from the fireworks, telling her he loved her. She wouldn't get that kind of service from Gary, he wouldn't even tell her if he *thought she was rather nice.*

"Mr. Swallow will see you now."

"Thank you for squeezing me in."

"You're welcome." They even said it in banks now. It was a new form of punctuation.

"Please take a seat." As if he would have stood.

"Thank you. I've come about increasing my overdraft."

"It's normal on these occasions to ask why."

Dermot felt sorry for bank managers. They had to hear this all the time. It was no way to spend your days.

"It's a temporary measure."

"Can you be more specific?"

"It's a temporary personal measure."

"I need more to go on."

"Why?"

The manager sat back in the soft leather and swiveled slightly. Dermot guessed that when Swallow was on his own he kicked off his shoes and swiveled all the way round. Men are boys.

"It's the bank's money."

"Where would you be if nobody wanted to borrow it?" It was strange how coy and also waspish they could suddenly be about usury.

"I'm sure there will always be someone who wants to. Personal bankruptcy is very distressing when it happens, as you can imagine."

"I've read my Dickens."

"The law has hardly changed." He consulted a sheet. "You already have a six hundred pound overdraft."

"Is it that much?"

"Are you in employment?"

"Yes, I work in a shop."

He paused and leaned close. The nearer you were to somebody the bigger their nose looked. "That's not very encouraging, is it. Working in a shop."

"I realize it's less lucrative than armed robbery."

"Apparently."

Dermot decided to tell a story.

"Alright I'll tell you what the money's for."

"I'd be grateful."

"There's a young lady upstairs who needs money."

"You also have urgent debts. I don't know how we gave you such a free rein."

"Her debts are urgenter. She thinks maybe two or three hundred pounds would do the trick."

"A word of advice Mr. Povey."

"Please call me Dermot."

"Don't mix pleasure and business. They are oil and water."

"I suppose she could get by with one hundred and fifty."

"No."

"You're right, she really needs the whole three hundred."

"Nothing."

"So little?"

"Nothing. And I want to see your existing overdraft reduced. Are you carrying your bank card with you?"

Dermot left the bank without his card. Clearly a defeat.

He had intended to spend his way into Deborah's affections, but only because that was what she asked him to do. She seemed to see it as an elementary test of his sincerity. If he passed she would perhaps be prepared to share Dermot's low life. Now he looked likely to fall at the first hurdle. In other contexts this was the best place to fall because it saved jumping any hurdles for nothing.

The suburbs of North London looked unusually shamefaced. Rain.

He walked the good walk home, noting the rhythm of the scenery, houses, shops, houses, shops. They called it a *parade* of shops, a laughable collocation in these parts. It was the season of pitching paving stones, after the recent waters, and Dermot twice twisted his ankle and douched his other foot on the unruly flags.

In one street there was a lonesome lamp burning at the top of its dog-rubbished post, a single star that had betrayed the centralized switch-throwers. It probably went out at lighting-up time, its life the eternal negative of its peers.

In a treelined avenue an elderly lady emerged from her garden carrying a jar of pickled onions and passed them into Dermot's hands. Wordlessly, with a twitch of her hands, she urged him to undo the jar, which he did with a slight grimace to indicate full commitment. A little of the vinegar skipped across the back of his hand and fell onto the damp pavement. The only commentary she gave was "Arthritis!" pronounced in a grievous whisper. She returned inside.

The patois of the streets was the muffled sound of residents banging around in their kitchens and the cries of children and birds laying on a squawky descant. The curbs were crowded with files of cars which had loops of seat belts snaking out under hurriedly closed doors and patches of cancered metal which blistered and darkened the paint. The vehicles themselves were of no interest to Dermot but he liked to glance inside at the human evidence they contained. Boxes of tissues and sunglasses, you found a lot of these. Road atlases with the pages bloated and yellow from the damp, tartan rugs, tins of travel sweets that were welded together inside, mud on the floors, dogs asleep.

Now that he had a day to spare Dermot was lost in all the vacant hours. He had been getting used to shoehorning his life into minutes and seconds. Arriving home, he sat in the kitchen and waited for the fine drizzle to evaporate from his hair. It would have been quicker to use a towel but there was no hurry.

He made himself a sandwich and sat at the table worrying about money. His poverty was not a matter of pride, he was ashamed of it. When he had no money as opposed to minus money he used for a time to call himself a minimalist and rail at the hoarders, the *possessed* as he called them because they were in the pay of their possessions (maintenance and dusting and waiting for them to break or lose themselves). But now that Dermot had bought himself an overdraft—a deep red, self-propelling machine—he could not afford to shout at the materialists.

It was comforting in the kitchen with the rain suddenly falling in sheets against the window and the low ceiling light throwing a soft cone over the table in the center of the room. When Dermot was a boy he used to spend long hours in his wardrobe. Smaller still, he was the only child he knew to put extra dividing walls into his Wendy house. So he was happy in his pool of enclosing light, shut off from the rain. He put the radio on, a trick he had learned from Gary, and listened to the Afternoon Play, very low.

The rain lifted or rather stopped falling, which is less spectacular. Dermot thought about money again and started to walk around the kitchen table. The orbits brought some inspiration. He decided to sell something. There was nothing of his in the kitchen and nothing salable in the hall. This was London, where there was no space, so they had no living room (they didn't sit in the kitchen because they loved kitchens, they sat there because that was where the chairs were). There was nothing salable in his bedroom or in his pockets. He had no rings on his fingers.

"And yet I'm not extravagant," he said to the walls.

Gary was the bearer of bitter laughter. During the day he re-lived the evening before. This brought on the bitter laughter. He'd taken Deborah to a restaurant because he had thought of no surprises, they being an alien currency. She had been off-hand. It so happened that being offhand was a subject Gary knew a good deal about because, of course, he had been it many times himself over the years and only recently cut down (it used to make him angry when he was described as an angry young man, such a cliché, but that's what he was). If she had done her homework she would have chosen a subject he was unfamiliar with like humility or physics. She was not even very good at being offhand, to his way of thinking.

She had hardly said anything to him, things like that. She had been charming and tactful with the sullen waitress and sullen with him. She ferried monosyllables across the table and sat watching the other couples touching fingers and hatching plans around them in the near-darkness. He had fought hard to set the meal alight with all manner of provocative and *humorous* comment.

"It's very dark in here," she said at one point, interrupting Gary in the middle of a provocative comment, "but I can still count at least five bosses trying to seduce their secretaries."

It was fair enough. Gary did not have the sole rights to provocation.

"The men are probably the secretaries," he replied. She ignored that and got on with dropping her bomb.

"The things girls have to do to get a free meal."

Gary let the conversation lapse after that. He was actually

a little numb. The big problem was his infatuation. In normal circumstances, in the absence of infatuation, he would have ripped into her. He would have made a bit of a scene. The whites of his eyes would have shone and there would have been other anger symptoms. But because of this infatuation he did nothing except go quiet and feel, if anything, that he would rather like to cry, just like his old dad.

There was another shocking moment when they had arrived home and as Gary was framing words of regret she said in all earnestness "When are we going out again?" It might have sounded like a challenge or a piece of wickedness but she kept her eyes steady and waited for an answer.

"Saturday."

"Alright, Saturday."

As if he didn't have enough problems with her, now she was depriving him of hopelessness. She was probably being calculatedly irrational but there was a small chance that she had got over her misbehavior and would be kind and thoughtful the next time. What really worried him was that he wanted to go out with her so much that she could do what she liked. If she asked him to put his hand in a fire for her he would put his hand in a fire. What if she *asked* him to?

"Good night last night?"

"Not bad thanks, George."

"Did she put up a fight?"

"It's not like that."

"When you young people feel like doing it you just do it. That's it, isn't it?"

"No that's not it. And I don't really count as young any more. Young is seventeen or eighteen."

"Not when you're fifty-six. As you get older, you describe more and more people as young. In a few years I'll think fifty-six is young, I know I will."

"It is young," Gary said.

"Seventeen or eighteen, you just said."

"Well who wants to be that age?"

"Everybody. I do. I know my wife does."

78

"Yeah actually I do too. You're probably right about everybody."

He broke off to serve a customer, an eighteen-year-old as it turned out, or close enough. He did not seem to be appreciating his age, but philatelists were not representative—they didn't get much fresh air, Geraldine was right, so they often looked unhappy. Gary gave him an album to look through and in due course money changed hands. Young people had money nowadays. They usually kept the notes screwed up like litter at the bottom of their trouser pockets. The older generation gave themselves away by cosseting their money in leather.

"It's not like that," he resumed. "I'm serious about this relationship, George."

"Is this the one that wants surprising the whole time?"

"That's right."

"I don't like the sound of that. Find yourself a girl with a head on her shoulders."

"She's got a head on her shoulders."

"You know what I mean."

Dermot stepped outside as it was getting dark. Soon he would have to start doing something about Gerald because he felt responsible. It was a job for the police but he knew that sometimes they were busy. How do you go about looking for a person? He would ask if there was a book about it in the library. In America, he heard, an incredible number of people got lost every year but it was a much larger country, more places to get lost in. A lot of the time it was children, stolen from pavements like tins from the shelf of a supermarket, but in some cases perhaps many it was fairly normal adults walking out of unsatisfactory lives and into the prospect of better ones.

Sentimental, Dermot. Missing persons, he knew, were in many perhaps most cases dead. That was why they were missing.

The rain had settled in for the evening. If November carried on like this the radio would soon be saying it was the wettest month since records began. It was always the wettest or the driest or the coldest month.

"Don't I know you?" Mike said at the front gate.

"Deborah's not in." He was looking self-assured and still had the threatening shoulders.

His kind of build wasn't the thing nowadays, not willowy enough. Traditional physical prowess of his kind was frequently looked on as an indication of vacuousness now. The hunger artists and the sick-at-heart had all the intelligence that was going.

"Not in. Really," he said.

"Really not in." Dermot was afraid but he was glad Mike was a big man. He would have hated to be beaten up by a small man.

"I know. I've been hanging around."

"You poor thing. You must be cold and wet."

Mike didn't like that. He pushed Dermot to the ground with his right hand. Dermot was tempted to stay right there on the damp concrete where he could not be knocked over again. He deserved to be there after saying that. Dermot would have done the same.

"Don't say stupid things."

"Don't do stupid things. If I want to sit down I'll do it myself."

"I think you should get up."

"I'm reasonably happy where I am."

Even so he got to his feet and Mike moved forward and pushed him again hard on the chest with the flat of his hand. This time Dermot almost stayed upright but eventually lost his balance and fell among cabbages. Geraldine grew a cabbage or two in her front garden the way most people grow flowers. He landed more softly than before but felt that much more silly, this being the second time.

"I thought I said get up."

"So I'm disobedient."

Although he was still afraid he was also exhilarated. Fighting (not that he had started yet, he would in a minute) was just another dangerous sport. Pugilism had a long and honorable history. Greeks, and so on.

"How do you think this is going to help you?" Dermot said as he got up. It sounded lame. It was better if you didn't talk.

"You got right up my nose yesterday. You and your squashy bearded friend. Especially him."

Dermot didn't bother to join in. (He was interested in the description *squashy*. Squashy was good.) He was examining the feasibility of running away over the low brick wall and then down the street. Though he imagined he would get away alright he worried about disposing of the stigma afterwards. On the other hand he liked the way his face was arranged. He didn't want teeth taken away or tiers added to his nose. There was a long and honorable history of running away.

As Dermot decided to run Mike turned to go.

"I've got nothing against you. Just tell Deborah she's coming back to me."

"You made her unhappy."

"I want her home."

Home. He wouldn't have expected a word like that from the kind of man who knocks you over. Also it was good to hear that Mike had nothing against him. At this rate Dermot would finish up getting quite fond of Mike.

But that random way that violent and disturbed men have made it difficult for him to leave just like that. Dermot could see that he was casting around for a way to say goodbye.

He went to the gate and pulled it off its hinges, leaving two stumps of metal edged with filaments of white wood. Dermot ran at him. Mike looked surprised but not alarmed, but Dermot didn't remember much because the rage had blinded him. He landed a bang with his fist and a kick but there wasn't enough weight in either. His fists in particular were a disappointment, and later when he looked at them he could see they were on the small side. Mike was hampered in the early stages by the fact that he still had the gate in his hands. It was unfortunate from Dermot's point of view that Mike had chosen to vandalize the gate because Gerald had fixed it recently and Gerald was a sensitive issue to say the least. If he had thrown a brick through a window Dermot would probably have let him get away with it because sometimes men like Mike need to let off steam. They need to externalize their tensions. Classical therapy encourages them to take up vigorous or dangerous sport, so Mike was halfway there with this pugilism, but energetic vandalism often did the trick just as well.

They scrapped and scraped around in silence (they didn't tell each other *take that!* they didn't even grunt very much but towards the end Dermot was in the mood for a soft groan).

Mike levered Dermot off with the gate and threw it at him. It fell across his knees and it hurt. He needed those knees. It was true what they said, the real pain coming later, but for the time being he had pain enough. Mike took part more actively in the next clinch, gathering Dermot up in one arm and slapping him twice round the face with his free hand. It was a curious, chastening gesture. Dermot kicked again, got free and went seriously mad.

Gary didn't suffer from nosebleeds but Dermot always had. As a boy he used to bleed spontaneously on buses and trains and whenever he was very nervous. Much of his childhood was spent in one remedial position or another waiting for his hemorrhages to pass. In the course of those years he tried them all: head between knees, head thrown back (he could feel the warm blood dripping down his throat), outstretched with his feet in the air, fingers on the bridge of his nose, on the end of his nose, hot and cold compresses. They had discussed cauterization but the truth was that Dermot's bleeding nose was a source of pleasure to him. It was what he did. In a big family like his you needed to specialize.

So when Gary arrived home and found Dermot nursing a persistent nosebleed he couldn't offer any technical assistance. He couldn't help noticing that Dermot had a slightly broken face and that his clothes were wet and torn but he was remarkably cheerful. Dermot told him he'd been in a fight.

"You little terror."

"It was Mike."

"The minute my back's turned." Gary was thinking: I

suppose I'm next. And I'll be expected to do better, because I'm taller. "Where does it hurt?"

"Most places."

"Shall I call a doctor?"

"Dough."

"Why are you squeezing your nose?"

"It's one of the suggested remedies."

It eventually stopped and Gary brought a bowl of hot water over to the table to sponge him down.

"I don't think anything's broken. You look symmetrical."

"I'm worried about one of my teeth."

"What's wrong with it?"

"It's in the garden."

"Open."

Dermot opened his mouth. It was an anxious little mouth with a quivery tongue. A single tooth had sheared off at the front to one side at a rakish angle.

"You'll have to get that capped."

"No I think I'll leave it as it is. Like the Getty boy with the ear."

"Without the ear."

"I don't think I hurt him you know."

"You're supposed to say You should see the other guy."

"Is that so."

Blood dries hard and it would have been more effective to wait for it to dry and then brush it off, but Dermot appreciated the care Gary showed and the warmth of the sponge.

9th

Gary was going to be late for work but there was nothing for it.

"I've come about two things," he said. "The first—"

The policeman had walked away to answer the telephone. He talked into the mouthpiece less than the earpiece talked to him, in fact he just said Yes, Yes, Yes for several minutes. Gary looked at the crime prevention posters. There was a missing person on one wall, a young ginger girl with an inappropriate smile. He wondered how they chose her from all the other missing persons. There were none of the modular Identi-Kit photographs that reminded Gary of cubist painting. The thieves on the prevention posters all had long lank hair and were probably recruited from a model agency, from the *ugly*-portfolio where they kept the photogenic grotesques, fat ladies and men with cadaverous faces.

"Let's try again."

"Yes. I've come about two things. The first involves a missing person who has been reported recently under the name of Gerald Jones. I want to help as far as possible and I wondered in what way I could assist your inquiries."

"It's been reported, then."

"Yes. I expect you've tapped his name into one of those computers you have."

The man looked at him sharply.

"We do use computers, yes sir, on occasions."

"In what way do you think I could assist your inquiries,

then?" He was trying to use the right vocabulary.

"I don't know the case in question but normally it's a matter of waiting. Obviously nobody has been picked up answering his description."

"The difficulty is in the waiting. Is there no plan B?"

"There are levels of inquiry. Waiting by the telephone is the most important thing in the early days. It's important to tell as many people as possible, inform all relatives and friends. But I assume all this has been done."

"Yes."

Gary had a mixed impression of the police. In this respect he was unique among his acquaintances who either thought the police were licensed criminals or doing-a-difficult-job-well. Gary agreed with them both. If anybody was going to catch these rapists and burglars and muggers it was licensed criminals.

"If after five or six days he hasn't returned we will most certainly take further steps."

"I see." He supposed that would have to do. In the private sector he might have asked to speak to the manager, the hammer not the rusty nail, because everyone respects a man who goes to the top. If he did that here he'd be tapped onto the computer himself and no mistake. "The other matter is regarding an assault."

"When did you, er, carry out this assault? Heh heh."

"Oh very good." A laughing policeman. The telephone rang again and this time he made a fuller contribution to the conversation, which nonetheless still made no sense on its own, like one hand clapping.

"Trouble?" Gary inquired pleasantly on his return to the front desk. Normally people welcome the chance to talk about their work.

The policeman looked at him sharply again.

"What do you think? This is a police station."

"Right! Trouble's your business." Gary regretted coming. He could have been selling stamps. He felt guilty just walking through the door. "Anyway, a friend of mine has just been badly beaten up and we wondered if we should prefer charges."

"It's not likely to be in your hands. Is your friend injured?"

"He's not well."

"Do you know who did it?"

"Oh yes."

"Who did it?"

"I'd rather not say. Big man. I'd just like your professional opinion at this stage. Actually my friend's only bruised. One eye's quite puffy."

"I'm sorry to hear that."

"He has a dent or two on his shins."

"It's up to him if he wants to talk to someone about it here."

"He has a chipped tooth."

"To be honest if everybody that got into a fight filed for assault we'd all be on twenty-four-hour shifts."

"Really, it's that common is it?"

"Very common."

"I'll tell my friend that, then."

Dermot had spent a peaceful night on the whole. It would have been more peaceful, for example, if he had not been beaten up the night before. But generally speaking he was not complaining. There was nobody at home so he couldn't complain, except by telephone.

There were some unsatisfactory aspects to this affair. There was the pain. There was the fact that Deborah had been out all night (that was extremely unsatisfactory) and the fact that today was payday but he couldn't go to work, the state of him.

He had forgotten what pain was like (it was painful). The aches and stabs. The throbbing, which was bad enough, and the nausea, which was *too* bad.

Where had Deborah been? Mike may have her, but he didn't know where she worked so that was unlikely. Let's face it, she was with another man. He wanted her to see him at his worst and she had been off peeling down her knickers in somebody else's bedroom.

"Personnel."

"Personnel?"

"Personnel."

"Good, I'm afraid I won't be coming in today." There was a pause, while Personnel came to terms with his disappointment.

"Who *are* you, then?"

"Don't snap, I'm not well. That's why I'm not coming in."

"The store employs hundreds of people. What's your name and your department?"

"Dermot Povey. Books. Formerly of electrical and kitchenware."

"What's the matter with you?"

"I was attacked."

"Will you be in tomorrow?"

"Will you?"

"No."

"In that case I will be in."

People were becoming ruder. And they didn't believe what you said anymore. Nobody wanted to make a fool of themselves nowadays by using up any of the small amount of trust they came into the world with.

He hobbled from the hall into the bathroom and ran hot water into the bath. While he waited he examined his body in the full-length mirror (until he lost definition under the merciful condensation). He didn't look good. He could go a little way sympathywise, on those injuries. Going seriously mad had been a mistake because a limb that flails is sooner or later going to meet a solid object and Mike had been solid. Although he couldn't remember too well he imagined Mike had picked off his lunges, which were lacking in science and also artless, like he was removing fluff from a jacket. Dermot's body bruises were gray on white and they hummed when he climbed into the hot water.

Dermot had never been one for singing in the bath but today he found himself intoning a Negro spiritual as he lay in the clear heat.

He washed his light brown hair—he still called it *blond* on official forms because that had been its color when he was a child—and soaped his hairless torso above the waterline. All the while the tip of his tongue played with the altered tooth.

Dermot dressed with care and closed the door behind him, first checking his face in the hall mirror. Some people were enhanced by grazes and bruises. On this evidence he was one of the unenhanced.

Deciding to walk although he felt as stiff as steel, Dermot had mothers and small children hugging the opposite side of the pavement, because of his puffy eye. It was still possible to scare and appall even in these times, when everyone is an old cynic and has seen far too much.

He climbed onto a bus after an ankle of his developed a click and a spasm.

"Where did you get that eye?"

"My wife." The conductor didn't believe him.

"It makes a change from husbands."

"That's why I let her do it."

"Have you tried raw steak on it?"

"What good does that do?"

"I don't know."

The woman sitting behind him leant forward and put a reassuring hand on his shoulder, left it there for three stops.

Deborah's sandwich bar was quiet at this time of the morning and the glass counter was bricked up with rolls and sandwiches.

"Where did you get that face?" she said.

"Guess," he said.

"Mike."

She asked for a few minutes off and was allowed to walk out with Dermot. They stood in the sunshine.

"I thought something like this would happen."

"Oh you did, did you. Where were you last night?"

"With a friend."

"Well obviously." She still had on her nurse's uniform—white for hygiene—and looked like an angel with the sun behind her head.

"You let somebody buy you a drink and they expect the key to your diary," she told him. "It was a girl."

"A friend of yours did this as well. I'm worried about your friends, Deborah."

"Lovers are not friends."

"Wait, let me write that down before I forget it."

"I have to go back now."

"Can I meet you after work here?"

"Six o'clock," she said and went back.

"Angelface," he said, but was not sure anymore. She had not been sympathetic.

It felt very wrong after what had happened but Gary was in an expensive shop buying Deborah a present. He should have been buying Dermot one—a sumptuous medical accessory—but this was the real world where forces other than fair-mindedness were in operation. Dermot in turn should have stepped aside and left Deborah to him. Dermot made friends easily and had no trouble making them into lovers while he, Gary, only got involved when he, Gary, was serious or in the last phase of sexual malnutrition. Gary, he, charged Dermot with stealing his girl. There was something about King David in this connection, if he remembered. David stole someone's wife although he had a *multitude* of his own. It was all there in those old stories.

What did women want? There were a lot of things even Gary knew that you didn't buy for a woman you had just met.

"Do you know the lady's size?"

"Small."

"What color?"

"White."

"The palest we have is yellow or eggshell blue."

"I thought you meant her skin. I want a dark jumper."

"How about navy?"

"That's blue isn't it?"

"Yes. Or green."

"Navy is blue or green?"

"No, no. We also have green."

"I like the idea of red."

"Burgundy or vermilion?"

"Don't you have red?"

Gary settled for black and arrived at work two hours late.

"The boys are talking, you know."

"You know how it is with boys, George."

"They think you're throwing yourself away on some woman."

Gary had never got close to the stallholders apart from George, who was a good and benign companion. On the other side, to his left, Gary had a Rumanian émigré who spoke as much English now as he did when he escaped with a sack of stamps and a low-fidelity phrasebook just after the war. He was not a great talker even in Rumanian. The others didn't have much in the way of urgent conversation, because they had abandoned themselves to imaginative albeit accurate theories about Gary's life.

"Have you been repeating our conversations?"

"No, you give yourself away. You had such regular habits."

"It might be anything. I could have been out on business."

"You used to do all that in your spare time. You were out every evening harrying old widows to sell."

"Only some evenings. I was young and greedy. Anyway it's *all* spare time, that's what self-employment means."

"You used to say that any time you weren't working you were losing money, that's what self-employment means. I can hear you saying it now."

"I go along with that logic, it's impeccable, but there's another logic which says that money has no value in itself."

"I've heard that one."

George went back to his tabloid but Gary wanted to talk.

George was the only person he could talk about Deborah with, apart from Deborah.

"What made you fall in love with your wife, George?"

"I wouldn't say I fell in love with her. I was happy in her company."

"She had a company did she?"

"I thought you wanted a serious talk."

"Sorry." George was getting shrewd about flippancy. Gary worried he might have cracked the code. "How could you tell you'd fallen in love?"

"I told you I didn't."

"Alright, when did you realize you were happy in her company?"

"I can't remember. I think they're right, though, you've fallen badly for this girl. Listen to you."

Gary felt that was enough. He'd had enough, he didn't want to talk about it anymore. He'd seen Dermot talking himself out of situations before, losing interest within a matter of hours simply by blabbing on about a loved one, who became used and exhausted as a result of her constant appearances in Dermot's purple passages. You could kill people by talking about them. (Admittedly, the opposite also happened and Dermot persuaded himself he liked someone he didn't like, and then he felt awful in the morning.) In spite of the bother his involvement was causing him Gary didn't want to talk himself out of being crazy about Deborah just yet.

He wondered how evenly Dorothy was matched with her new man. You saw some shocking mésalliances walking the pavements. He and Dorothy had looked about right for each other but that didn't mean they were. Sometimes a couple might look unlikely, like he and Deborah, and get along fine.

He stayed at his stall through lunch and worked hard all afternoon making money, although it had no value in itself.

After work he walked briskly across town to where Deborah said she worked, carrying the cashmere jumper in its slippery plastic bag.

It was raining again and there was an atmosphere of panic as there always was on a Friday. The weekend was already running out. Soon it would be Monday.

Gary knew he had arrived when he saw Dermot standing on the pavement. He was being buffeted by the rush hour.

"You should be home in bed."

"It's you."

"Shit, Dermot."

"What?"

"You should be home in bed."

"Don't keep saying that. What's this *shit, Dermot* business?"

"Can't you leave Deborah alone? Look where it's got you."

"I thought we'd have all this out in the open sooner or later."

Dermot's eye didn't look puffy any more. A little fat perhaps. The graze on his cheek was brown while this time yesterday it was a liquid red grid. Gary was tempted to hit him again before it healed.

"I want to take her out."

"Don't be ridiculous Gary, that's not how it goes. Things don't happen just because you want them to."

"Yeah?"

"Yeah."

We're all yobs, Gary and Dermot realized separately. Scratch a decent man and you find yob.

Gary checked his tie for straightness and went in. A man called out, "We're closed."

"It's okay, I've already eaten."

Deborah and a man with a cigarette in his mouth were sweeping up and wiping down.

"Deborah. I've bought you something."

She looked perturbed for a moment and unclear whether to take it. "What is it?"

"Does it make a difference?"

They both glanced through the window and saw Dermot

looking in with his brow furrowed. The sign on the door said Open, meaning Closed.

"Who's your monkey?"

"I was just about to ask you."

She opened the bag and held the jumper up.

"Is it your size?"

She held it closely over her. Outside, Dermot frowned more deeply at the dumb show. He wanted more light. Her hands cupped her breasts and she seemed to look at him challengingly. He wanted more light on her, floodlights.

"It seems to be," she answered. Gary was looking at her eyes to see how tired she was. It had not escaped him that last night she had been away. Three times he had climbed her stairs.

"Good. I gather you're going out with Dermot tonight."

"Is that what he told you?"

"How else would I know?"

"He's standing there."

"He always does a lot of hovering in the early stages while he still has his enthusiasm."

"I don't suppose you're one to hover. Correct me if I'm wrong but you're down for tomorrow night."

She was enjoying herself and much as Gary liked to see her happy he most of all liked to be happy himself. "It's not funny, this situation," he said. "It's making me miserable."

"I can take it or leave it myself. I shouldn't think it will last."

Gary left without mentioning Mike or the police. She wasn't looking tired, in fact she wasn't looking anything he could identify.

Outside Dermot edged up to him nervously and asked to borrow some money. He lent him twenty pounds and went home.

He arrived feeling wet and desolate, not wanting to spend the evening in because nothing could possibly happen except maybe Mike would come round and want to tattoo his body with his fist.

He knocked on Geraldine's door and sat with her and Gwen. They were a sad couple—with Gwen it was congenital and with Geraldine it was because her husband had been missing for three days. He tried to cheer them up by telling them the story of Dermot's eye but they only nodded and said that it was an evil world. He told them about his chat with the policeman, to show that he was concerned and not standing idly by. He lied to them that he had been into quite a few pubs in the hope of finding Gerald nibbling at a tomato juice. There was nothing he could say and everything he could not say (about men and death, about the past because it had memories of Gerald and the future because it was black).

Gwen made him laugh. She was pessimism's watchdog, barking at hope or levity. In the last three days she had had to restrain her urge to yap and growl lest she drive Geraldine all the way to suicide. She didn't think much of Gary, he knew, but that was how much she thought of everyone. Her husband went away to sea most of the time but apparently he did that even before they met.

The television talked to itself in the corner of the room. Gwen stole terse glances at it and Geraldine listened out vaguely in the hope of hearing about Gerald—it was common knowledge that the newsgatherers were quicker than the police. They had their deadlines while the police had nothing to spur them on but a stale sense of duty. Even so, the television had nothing to say about Gerald, unless he was on another channel. In between their broken exchanges Gary scanned the room for a clue to why Gerald had disappeared. It could have been the curtains.

There was a scene every time the telephone rang, Geraldine getting there first (Gwen a victim of motor empathy) while Gary went to turn the television down low. It was an old black-and-white set and had a volume knob the size of a baby's fist. The calls each sounded more urgent than the last. Once Geraldine shouted "That's his ring, I know it is" but it turned out to be Gerald's brother in Halifax, Nova Scotia, so only consanguinity would account for the similarity of the ring.

Every time the caller was someone other than Gerald, which was every time, the skin above Geraldine's eyes sagged further over her eyelids. Her face was being attacked from the inside by thoughts.

Three or four programs came on and before each one Gary said "I really have to go" but stayed. When he had a television of his own he was the same. He was always there to hear them tell him to switch off the set and sleep well.

They made the tea in rotation. Gary was least happy when Geraldine made it and left him alone with Gwen.

"She's bearing up well, isn't she."

"Not really."

She sat with her hands clasped over her stomach. Gary wondered where her husband was. Perhaps if he'd taken his wife with him, shown her Jakarta and the Golden Gate Bridge and Tahiti, she would have been a different woman, running off her gloom on a distant beach under palm fronds. Gerald had no history of seafaring even across the Channel so he was likely to be in the country still, in one form or another, although one peculiarity of his was a soundtrack of waves crashing against a beach, which according to Geraldine he used to play regularly a few years back.

When it was Gary's turn to make the tea he spent an extra few moments cleaning up the kitchen and polishing the taps. He brought the pot in on a silvery tray, set it down with a flourish and, without meaning to, said, "Now. Shall I be father?"

"I don't have Gary's money, you see."

"You just told me you did."

"I mean I don't have as *much* as him. I borrowed a little for this evening. Personally I just think his buying you presents puts him into the same basket as Mike. Money is a form of violence. It gets you stuff you don't deserve."

"I'm stuff, am I?"

They were sitting in a pub again but were going to see a film which Deborah had chosen. He considered it an honor to

95

be with her even though she was wearing Gary's black cashmere.

"Deborah, I don't want to argue. I love you."

"Mike used to say that, the last part anyway."

"What are you trying to say?"

"Nothing."

"I don't use those words lightly. I don't *use* those words."

"I'm not looking for a phrase. Phrases are cheaper than money and get men stuff they don't deserve."

"Very slick."

They saw a disaster movie involving a plane that had crashed in the desert. The actors' verbal dexterity was hampered by their badly cracked lips. Dermot couldn't believe Deborah wanted to see a film like this except to punish him, but she looked rapt whenever he caught her profile. His own mind drifted. He crossed and uncrossed his arms more than he should. More than once he glanced down at her legs but, fearing her resentment, allowed himself less time than he needed to drink in their shape.

In the film the bad and old people died whereas the young and good collapsed into the arms of Bedouins. A blue-black Nubian treated their cracked lips with annealing herbs and unguents.

Dermot liked the darkness of cinemas in winter and he liked to hear laughter rattling around the auditorium. He enjoyed sex films but nobody he knew admitted to that so he kept quiet too. What he hated was the clammy boredom that fell upon him one third into many films and the awful worry that the cinema might catch fire. He had fire dreams. He checked exits when he arrived, like a man on the run.

Like many boys who had become men now Dermot had, under the cover of cineramic darkness, put his hand into the clothes of young female companions and stretched and strained his fingers into gratifying places. Breasts felt cold and thighs were hot. He didn't care what films he saw in those days because there was always more plot and craft where he was sitting.

"How was it for you?" he asked afterwards.

"Not bad. How was it for you?"

"I would have enjoyed it more if I was aching less."

They walked along the crowded streets where cineastes in stained anoraks elbowed or were elbowed by theatergoers with hickory-handled unbrellas. The pleasurehouses were being evacuated calmly.

Dermot put his arm into Deborah's and was not surprised when she lifted it from her and wedged it back into his pocket. He thought she did it gently and almost with regret but he had been wrong before.

"You should have run away from him," she said, at length.

"You didn't."

"I did."

"You took your time," he said.

"I was used to rough men. I told you my dad ran a pub. His pub didn't have horse-brasses and cocktails, it had men threatening each other."

Dermot had a bad ear (it also ached) and he didn't listen out much for accents, nor was he much of a sociologist. Even so, she didn't sound like she'd grown up in spit and sawdust, serving stout to the bottom rung. She'd gutted the working class from her voice and bourgeois vowels had moved in.

"Men threaten each other in wine bars. They get drunk and disobedient in yacht clubs and golf clubs."

"I wouldn't know."

"Alright so you had a tough upbringing. Where did you learn to speak like the BBC?"

"Probably from the BBC."

"Why?"

"Maybe I thought I'd meet some chartered accountants this way. That's what Mike wanted to be when he was at school."

"Too bad."

Deborah allowed a pause to fall so that she could ask "How did you meet Gary?" and ask it in such a way that suggested Gary was as intriguing an issue as she had ever come across.

"We've never met," he said, because it seemed an interesting thing to say. Then he paused, to show he could pause just as well as she could. "No, actually, I once pulled a thorn from his foot and now he follows me everywhere I go. No, I tell a lie. I got him in a garage sale." This was the approach Gary would have approved of—why be direct and sweet when you can be obscure and sour?

"It's not important. It was only a question," she said.

If you love somebody and want them to love you, he wanted to tell her, nothing that person says is ever *only a question*. It becomes *evidence*. Nevertheless, her two little sentences had made him feel cheap.

He explained: "We met at a squash club." This was a version of how they might have been perceived, observed down the wrong end of a telescope, to have met. The full circumstances, though perhaps no more interesting, said something about their personalities.

Dermot had joined the squash club in order to find an athletic girlfriend. He felt it would be advantageous, for instance, if she was able when they made love to put her ankles over his shoulders without complaining about her back. Gary had joined to play squash.

Dermot had his nose pressed up against the glass and was watching two women on the court below. He hoped they would look up at the spectators' gallery so that he could give them an erotic wave. Dermot remembered Gary's first words to him, spoken to his back as he tried to imagine what an erotic wave looked like.

"Are you Douglas Binns?" he had asked.

"No." The only possible answer.

"You're not Douglas Binns?"

Dermot finally turned round. "No. Are *you* Douglas Binns?" Gary reminded him of a ship's purser. It was his beard and his immaculate blue squashwear.

"He's above me on the squash ladder."

"What's a squash ladder?"

Gary explained how it worked in minute detail ("Do you want me to go over that again?") and insisted that Dermot would benefit from the structure it imposed on the squash player's game. Dermot made the spectacular claim that competitiveness had no place in sport but Gary brushed this aside and arranged a game for them. They were well matched as players but Dermot lost points for appearing on court without socks and in a tattered T-shirt reminiscent of seaweed.

Dermot had trouble pinning Gary's personality down. At first there was a crazed solemnity about his expression which suggested that the lift did not go all the way up to the top floor. Was this the club idiot whom nobody would play with? Just as Dermot was about to make his excuses and leave—his favorite line at that time was "Excuse me, I have to go over to the other side of the room"—he noticed a sly wit at the edge of Gary's eye, glimmering through the dry nonsense of Douggie Binns. He had the low monotonous voice of a man who is speaking through bandages. He was pompous. He kept his squash racket in a press and his squash socks in a plastic bag with a label on it marked Squash Socks and underlined. Nonetheless, Dermot felt, let's give the boy a chance. Let's get it out of its box and see if it's a real person.

"Relationships are born by Chance out of Mutual Convenience," Dermot once told an impressionable girlfriend whom he had met when he worked in a bookmaker's. The convenient feature about Gary was that he was looking for somebody to share his flat. Dermot's own landlord had never gone along with his relaxed approach to the concept of rent so he moved in with Gary.

"So that was how we met," he said eventually.

"You haven't explained how," Deborah replied.

"There's no need," he told her. "I've just been over it in my own mind."

10th

Saturday, Dermot and Gary met in the kitchen for their first breakfast together since the last time. They exchanged words about their respective evenings. Dermot thanked his friend for lending him money and his friend said that it was a pleasure and proceeded with an inquiry as to Dermot's health, telling him that he had been down to the police station to get advice.

Gary was in a better mood and fried a proper breakfast, with all the bits.

"They don't seem too bothered," he said as he watched the eggs spit. "Apparently fights are very common."

"This wasn't a fight. A fight implies mutual aggression, agreed in advance. It was only mutual on his side."

"Let's forget about it. We'll give him one more chance."

Dermot didn't mind. Gary was next in line. And Gary would be expected to do better than him, because he was taller and fatter.

"Never two without three," Dermot said. "He'll come here again to lay you out. I'm sure you'll cope."

It was Dermot's turn to have resentments. He didn't want Gary to go out with Deborah that night, he resented *that* arrangement. He felt oppressed by his failure to break her down and make their relationship sing a little. And what was Gary so happy about (they were on a happiness seesaw and couldn't both be up, although somehow they could both be down)? That was three fat resentments.

He arrived at work and stood among the books. His manager beckoned. "What have we here?"

"Black eye."

"Yes. How do you explain it?"

"It's a form of bruising. The blood vessels around the eye are loosely suspended, apparently, and bruise easily."

"Thank you. I think you understand what I'm saying."

"I was attacked in the street for money."

"That's awful." He was a charming man and didn't deserve these lies or any other kind.

"He didn't get any money."

"It was brave of you to fight him off."

"I didn't have any money on me."

"That's worse isn't it?"

"Yes, they hate poor people. They get furious when they don't find anything in your pockets."

Saturday was a busy day and there were plenty of staff who wanted to hear Dermot's short but marketable story. If he didn't have Deborah he would have taken this opportunity to make headway with till-girl Candice, who wore black nail varnish as if she'd shut her fingers in a car door. Or he might have approached Carolyn, who had these eyes, with a suggestion that they lose themselves in each other for the weekend.

The public weren't bothered with books that day. They were elsewhere. At midday Dermot was removed to the jewelry department on the ground floor which was under siege from customers who should have been upstairs buying books. Only full-time employees were allowed to work in Jewelry because Saturday staff had a reputation for larceny.

Dermot knew next to nothing about jewelry. It was somewhere to put your money if you already had a nice house and car. If he had any jewelry he wouldn't have worn it, because opulence often offends. It frightened him to see expensive earrings since he read about a man who ripped them out of pierced ears, leaving shredded lobes and the sound of screaming behind him. In Naples hard men lopped off fingers in the street rather than kill time unthreading reluctant rings from the hands of the well jeweled. Can you believe it? Most of the time you were safe in your gold, naturally, but it was as well to know the dangers. Dermot was alive to dangers now.

Special offers had made Jewelry into a bear garden. Temporary signs said there was money off this and money off that. Dermot took care of gift wrapping and for the first hour he turned out packages with flapping paper and dog-ears. Then he got better and quicker and his packages looked more like gifts and less like jokes.

He started to think about Deborah and that was when the nerve pains started in his stomach. They coincided with his decision to steal a necklace for her.

There were all kinds of reasons for not stealing.

He might get caught.

He might not get caught and get guilt instead. Dermot went along with the still widely held belief that you should not steal because stealing is wrong. *Wrong* was a big word, very large, but it was simpler to swallow it whole.

He had not stolen anything in his life so was under-rehearsed. It would be awkward as many things are the first time.

On the other hand there was this.

He might not get caught and feel just fine.

If he was caught (and his nervous ache surged when he thought about it) he could claim concussion and accelerated moral degeneration arising from shock.

It was *about time* he stole something. We only pass this way once.

And above all he wanted Deborah to see how far he would go. He didn't believe she was that interested in money but perhaps she was mixed up enough to want love tokens and tributes.

There was a blind corner under the counter where Dermot knew he would not be seen by colleagues or public. Just above there was a rack of necklaces of varying tastefulness, none so expensive that they would be remembered nor so cheap that he would look ridiculous if it came to court.

He changed his mind every minute for an hour and a half. When it finally happened the chain felt as light and dangerous as cyanide in his trouser pocket and he wondered if it was actually there. For a moment he expected to find it glistening on his shoe or dangling from a button, prior to being used in evidence against him. After a sensible delay he scanned his colleagues for knowing looks but their faces showed only tiredness because it was a bear garden. The last hour was a long one for Dermot. It had a hundred minutes or more in it. Sometimes they searched your bag on the way out of the shop because it is a well-known fact that some workers are tempted beyond endurance by the products they sell. There were those that called this profit sharing, but the general view was that internal theft was a bad thing and should be stamped out like cholera or hepatitis B. Dermot didn't have a bag but he did have voluminous pockets that could house anything from two or three pounds of carrots to a necklace. He therefore transferred the slinky gold chain from his pocket to his sock where the security men in green uniforms seldom dipped their hands.

That day, of all days, there were no green men in attendance and Dermot walked free.

He didn't feel good about himself.

Poor Dermot. It looked like he was getting nowhere. What a mood he'd been in that morning, sulky and frosty towards his eggs. It looked bad for him and Deborah, which was good for *him* and Deborah.

Gary wrestled with his chains.

"You should pack that lock with grease," George said.

Gary tried to turn the key again, loading his fingers with torque. "I know I bloody should. I bloody know." Somehow he knew he never would. Grease sellers were fat cats.

"You'll snap your wrist off."

"Unlikely."

Waggling freed it in the end and Gary pushed up the shutter, opened the safe, counted his money, went about his business.

"I have these stamps to sell," a boy said. They were in a white paper bag held by a rubber band. Gary remembered when he was a boy.

"You've come to the right place." He was young with a freshly broken voice. Gary used to come down to London when he was that age, escaping from Hertfordshire in a train with dirty windows, and loiter in these places with a thumbed catalog in his hand. His parents were out of touch even in those days and probably imagined he went to school on Saturday or had a woman in town, just like his father. They sedated him with big pocket money and he cheated them by investing it wisely. By the time he was eighteen Gary was in a position to offer pocket money to his own parents. The boy reminded him of himself but his attitude was different.

"Why are you selling them?"

"I just want the money."

"Sweet shop called in your debts?"

"I've lost interest."

Gary gave him fifty pounds and would probably sell them for forty. He'd lost interest too. He should change his trade before he got a taste for largess.

There was the evening to take care of and he wasn't keen to risk another restaurant. He didn't want Deborah making a meal of it like the last time. (Some people simply freeze up in formal situations such as candlelit dinners. It's not their fault.) He had bought a magazine that told you what was going on and how to enjoy yourself and he was flicking through its pages. How would she react to greyhounds? He'd never been to the dogs or been ice skating or ten-pin bowling. He would look gross in skates whereas she would glide and twirl and stick her arse out like a true professional when she took a fast corner. She would clean up on the bowling, too, and despise him. They could go to the cinema but the cinema was nothing.

"Where would you take a girl out in London, George?"

"You're asking the wrong man."

"I know."

"I'd start with the theater."

"I'm not sure I want to see a play."

"Whose evening is it, yours or hers?"

"We're going together. That's the whole point."

"She's more important, surely."

"You're right. I forgot what I was saying for a moment."

"And then I'd take her to a restaurant."

"Is that really necessary?"

"French."

"Alright."

"And then we'd go dancing."

"On a full stomach? You should understand that I always eat and drink for four."

"They like dancing. Women have natural rhythm, Gary."

"You're thinking of West Indians. Women have intuition."

"As I say, you're asking the wrong man."

"I know," he said again and then used the telephone to book two theater tickets and order a table.

Dermot continued to look over both shoulders for a long long while until, in time, cramp came upon the big muscle that ran from beneath his ear down his neck and into his shirt. The bus's air brakes hissed hatefully and startled Dermot as he sat with his guilt. The third time this happened he decided to take the chain back the next day. Unstealing was the hardest thing. It had surprise on its side, but stealing was better documented. Many shoplifters had regrets but they usually had them when they were arrested or sentenced. They didn't very often return goods they had stolen, unless they were the wrong size or the color clashed horribly with some other piece of pilfer. Dermot was a recidivist who relapsed habitually into honesty; he had no use for hot neckwear.

He climbed off the bus and changed his mind. Men stole for their well-beloved. They cheated other men and sacrificed their friends. They laughed off disinheritance, if absolutely necessary.

"Dermot, Dermot."

Geraldine held the door open for him and waved a piece of stiff card.

"Is Gerald back?" he asked, matching her animation.

She cooled a little at this. "No."

"But he's on his way?"

"He doesn't say."

It was true that she wasn't smiling, but she had come alive. Inside her pink and furry slippers Dermot could see her toes flexing excitedly.

She gave him the card and watched his face. He examined the legend *Greetings From Sussex* and the four green views. On the white side was Geraldine's address and name, written in an even, elegant hand. The postmark said Sussex Coast and dated itself Friday the 9th A.M. across the royal cheek. The half that mattered was light on information, reading

> I have gone away. Sorry.
> Don't worry I am fine.
> Take care. Gerald.

Dermot thought initially it was a poem because the layout of the words was tight in the center of the message box and had a considered and formal appearance. It was Gerald's copperplate and the dots of his i's hugged their stems in a sane, precise manner.

"It arrived this morning," she said. "The postman brought it," she added, as if sometimes it was the milkman.

"Thank God he's written. What would he be doing in Sussex?"

"I can't understand it. We don't know anybody down there."

"Have you ever been there together?"

"We've been to Brighton once or twice."

"Have a nice time?" he asked, lapsing into pleasantry.

"Oh yes. We went on the pier." A sheen fell across her eyes but she wiped the tears away with a single sweep of her hand. At that moment Dermot would have done anything to get Gerald home to his wife. He saw the two of them leaning on the painted railings of the pier, only a few years into their marriage, Geraldine ozone-drunk and disorderly, Gerald laughing and struggling to control the flapping of his trouser legs in the stiff breeze. Gerald had a pencil moustache and Geraldine had white high-heeled shoes which occasionally wedged themselves between the bleached planks as they walked, making them laugh each time.

And now they hardly spoke and Gerald was writing atmospheric but unhelpful postcards from an unknown address.

"What do you think we should do?" she asked in a fluttering voice.

"Wait for the next postcard. Wait for him to run out of money."

"It looks like he's on his own." That relieved her greatly.

"I wonder where he's staying. Have you found out about the postmark?"

She tried to concentrate. "The man at the post office said it was probably sorted in Brighton but it wasn't possible to say exactly where it was posted."

"That's unfortunate."

"Come in and have some tea."

He could not resist, though he wanted to. As they went through the kitchen she said after her, "That's a bruise on your eye isn't it?"

"Yes. I tripped over the carpet and hit my eye on a chair."

"I think Gary told me something about it last night. I'm afraid I wasn't listening."

"I try not to listen to him. Actually I was in a fight, but enough of my troubles."

It was sad that nobody had come to live with her in the last few trying days. Most people had a cousin or sister who loved an emergency. Dermot had a sister who, were he to lose a limb or his mind, would have dropped everything to sit with him for a year or so.

The ground-floor flat was gathering dirt. In the turmoil of life without Gerald Geraldine had lost the will to keep her house in order and her furniture had a soft look about it owing to the layer of damask dust. Gary had trained Dermot to notice dust in the course of their cohabitation (Dermot was influenceable) and he was now stuck with the dreary ability to tell exactly when a room was last dusted. He put this place at eight or nine days, which was by no means shaming.

"Have you spoken to the new girl?" she asked as she put the water on. It was the first time Geraldine had spoken about *nonrelated matters* since her husband started to monopolize conversations (by disappearing. That was the only way he could ever do such a thing). It was tough but she had done it.

"I've done more than speak to her. We've been out together."

"Out together?"

"Yes, you know. The cinema."

"Who's a naughty boy then?" she crooned, her old self.

"Gary is. He's been out with her as well."

"A love triangle," she said with the same concentration she always showed when trying to fit a technical term to real life.

"Except that only a third of us are in love." He didn't believe Gary really loved Deborah any more than he believed she loved Gary. Nor did she love him, Dermot, in *spite of the fact* that he, of course, loved her. That only left Dermot and Gary together and they were not sure they even liked each other. If there was triangularity it looked like this:

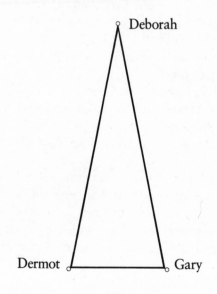

an isosceles pedestal. Gary was entitled to an equal footing with Dermot only because he had perhaps persuaded himself in all sincerity that he loved Deborah and this only abstractly, because Dermot's own passion had sown the germ in his head. Note how far the two men are from the female vertex.

The situation was not static. Dermot had chances still:

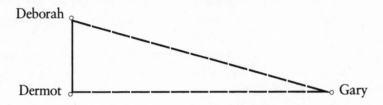

Gary could be squeezed out. He would quickly lose interest at the thin end of the wedge if Dermot could narrow the gap that separated himself from Deborah. Little things brought a man suddenly closer—a freak voluptuous aftershave, the right word at the right time. Women were susceptible to latent conversion, in his experience—by contrast there was not a lot a woman could hope for if she didn't impress her man straight-away across a crowded room.

Dermot went on doodling with Geraldine's phrase as the water boiled and splashed into the teapot. He was an optimist but only stayed that way by understanding that the worst was always happening:

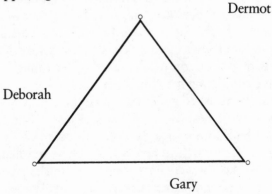

People drifted and the allegiances they built up were so much rain falling on the ocean. He would not leave Deborah but she could easily slip away.

"What are you thinking about, darling?"

"Gerald," he said. "No, no sugar." Gerald was more important at this stage.

"What do you think we should do?" she said for the second time. She was either forgetful, or waiting for an answer that suited her.

"It's not a police matter any more. We can't ask for sniffer dogs to be sent out across the South Downs. Are there any haunts he might visit?"

"The pier?"

"Motels he might stay in?"

"We only went for day trips."

"Well that's it then, we'll have to wait. Try to think about other things. Watch a lot of television."

Gwen arrived from next door with the corners of her mouth down by her knees. Geraldine seemed calm so he left her and went straightaway to Deborah.

She told him "Wait a second" when he knocked, so he stood and looked at her door. The sound of water gave way to silence. She had a small shower in a cupboard, cordoned off by a plastic curtain which swished when she jagged it open. "Ah. Come in."

She had put on her tracksuit over her damp body. Her hands and feet were wetly pink with pearl-white nails. She sat in front of the fire and rubbed her short thick hair with a towel. Dermot stood at her back and with her arms raised to her head Deborah showed him two inches of pale skin above her waistband, more aphrodisiac than the curve of a hundred naked thighs.

"I have something for you," he said.

"What?" she asked and went on rubbing.

He went down on one knee and hooked his finger around part of the chain in his sock. It wouldn't come easily so he sat down next to Deborah and removed his shoe and then his tired brown sock. She showed no surprise as he dangled his sock from the toe and shook out the bright booty. He examined it himself first and had to say that, random though it was, he had made a good choice—a chain with solid links and a pendant heart which though small was plump and almost lifelike, lacking only the stumps of arteries and veins. He expected it to pump and jump in his palm. He gave it to her.

"I thought you had no money."

"I stole it for you."

"Why?"

"I wanted to give you something."

"I didn't want anything."

"That's not what you said."

"You shouldn't believe what I say."

"Don't you like it?"

"I don't wear jewelry."

That was what she said, but Dermot distrusted her. She kept it in her hand.

"You shouldn't have done this," she warned severely. "Mike can do this kind of thing but you can't. People like you get caught."

"Not me. I'm like a cat."

"The authorities don't like it when the middle classes get light fingers. It confuses them."

It could be that he had made a mistake, but he noticed she wasn't giving him the chain back. He didn't enjoy these arguments about class. He never had been able to make a good case for bourgeois mores except to say that his parents had been concientious providers and they had never told him he was not to play with the children on the council estate.

"I have to get dressed now," she said, but didn't move. Dermot still had his sock off and their three bare feet lay together on the rug. She undid the catch, brought the chain up to her neck and joined the circle again with an efficient twist of her fingers. The zip down the center of her chest she teased open a little so that the heart could be seen. She rested her hands back on the carpet and looked at Dermot.

"Thanks."

He put his sock back on and then his shoe.

"I'll leave you to get dressed then."

"Yes."

"You'll want to look nice for Gary."

"What makes you think that?"

"What do you think of Dermot?"

"I like him," Deborah said. He gave her time to qualify *like* (But he irritates me. But let's face it he's a bit pathetic. But I like *you more*.) but she carried on sipping her soda water.

Was it bad manners, or what, for a woman to talk of great warmth for A when his best friend B was taking her out to the theater? Was B being unreasonable?

Do you like me more, less, or as much? That was the question that tripped on the heels of the last but he couldn't bring himself to ask it in case she said *I like you less*. A bald admission like that would do his evening no good at all.

Gary dreaded the interval because it always took a long time to get to the bar and when you did get there it was time to go back in and you couldn't take your drinks with you. For the first time in his life he had placed his order before the show began but he came back to find soda water instead of tonic water and he couldn't complain because he couldn't get to the bar. To make matters worse Deborah had not said, as he thought she should have, that soda water was just as good and he was not to worry, in fact she had more or less suggested she loathed soda water.

Going out was much more trouble than staying in.

An American musical was what it was and although it hurt to say so Gary had to admit it was a damn fine show, *damn* fine. The girls could certainly tap and they could do it in lines of twenty, no problem. He normally enjoyed a show more if he hated it because if he enjoyed it he would be encouraged to go to the theater again fairly soon and going out was much more trouble than staying in. After a while, fortunately, a lucky sequence of good plays always ended with some execrable drama that scared him away from the theater for a year or more. Meanwhile, Gary looked and knew he looked sober and even dignified in his beard and frown, but when the songs started and the dancing rolled across the stage he was prepared to admit he would have sold his soul for a place in the chorus.

Deborah liked the show too and they would have been in a happier frame of mind if they had discussed the first half. That was what the interval was for. They put it there in the middle of the proceedings specifically, rather than at the beginning or at the end. Instead he had mentioned Dermot, and Dermot wasn't even in the program.

"He gave me this," she said and released from the collar of her dress the heart.

"He hasn't got any money," Gary said, looking closely. "Or did it come free with breakfast cereal?"

"It's hallmarked."

"I'll have to have a word with him about this. It looks like he's been going through his mother's handbag. I've told him about it."

"I don't care where he got it from."

"I suppose you got used to not asking for receipts when you were living with Mike." This was in the gray zone between persiflage and mudslinging. He nearly said *I didn't mean that rudely.*

"I don't want to talk about him."

"Nor do I. Let's talk about Mike instead."

She sighed and the bell went to tell them they could all go back in now. Gary downed his lager impetuously and some trickled into his beard, which happened.

He should have been more discreet about the jumper he gave her. Dermot had taken it to be a gauntlet thrown down. Where did he raise the money and why, incidentally, wasn't she wearing the bloody jumper? It fit her like a glove. (It *was* a gauntlet, though. Dermot was right. Gary was challenging him to admit he should give up now and find a cheaper girl, one who could go without presents and who, when she went out of an evening, liked nothing more expensive than a walk in the park. He must find a woman he could afford to keep in a style to which she was accustomed, that is to say a poor woman.)

113

Gary didn't like the second half as much as the first half, but at least he had enjoyed the first. When the show was over and he was trying to find the restaurant, he hoped Deborah would tuck the heart back in her dress but she let it bounce instead in the open V of her raincoat. He led the way but kept looking back to check she was still there. He didn't know why she'd come out with him and was prepared constantly to find her gone.

"It's here somewhere."

"Have you been before?"

"Oh yes. I don't say the headwaiter knows me by name." He'd been there once with Dorothy, a rare outing, and the head-waiter had called him Mr. Shuttleworth, which was not his name.

Eventually Gary found the restaurant down a street it had not been before.

Deborah was more relaxed and amenable than when last they ate together, but this change could have little to do with him because he was no different from the last time, same suppressed truculence, same desire to please. He was self-assured in restaurants, a smooth companion except when he felt he had to complain and even this he did with a skill born of practice. This evening he sent a fork back to the kitchen to be washed and left it at that, although subsequently he discovered a smear on his spoon. He always ran a cutlery check and on those rare occasions when he was a guest at a dinner party he might slip out to the kitchen before the hors d'oeuvre and rinse a suspect fish knife in his hostess's water.

"Dermot's very unstable, did you know?" he asked when they had ordered. Gary considered it a pivotal moment, the question that followed the folding of the menus and the waiter's disappearance. It was then that business lunches took a heavy turn (What I had in mind was this.) and lovers made leading statements (Hugo, I think David's found out. You left your cufflinks behind the alarm clock).

"What makes you say that?"

"I've lived with him for two years and known him almost as long."

"What form does this instability take?" She didn't believe him.

"He changes jobs a lot. He's had eight this year."

"Why did he leave them all?"

"He's insubordinate. He takes badly to subordination."

"And yet he seems quite content."

"He's a master of disguise."

"What kind of jobs has he done?"

"What kind of jobs hasn't he done."

"I wonder why he's like that."

Don't make him sound interesting.

"I don't really care. I'm bored with it. There's enough un-employment around without him running amok using his fancy degree to get work he doesn't deserve."

The food came and broke up the conversation. As one ate, the other spoke. Gary sometimes tried both.

"What did you do before your present job?" he asked.

"Went to sandwich-making college," she said, keeping her face straight and then putting her fork into it. Whatever Gary ordered he always ended up wanting what the other person had. If Deborah had chosen tripe in acid he would have ended up wanting tripe in acid too.

"Okay, you ask the questions."

"I did a lot of jobs. I worked for Mike for a while."

"I bet they were queuing around the block to replace you when you left. What did you have to do, hold his coat? Drill holes in people's knees?"

"He's a successful businessman. He buys and sells."

"I won't ask what." He poured himself some wine and knifed some more flesh off the bone. "What?"

"Various things. Property, revolving bow ties."

"An entrepreneur. We need our entrepreneurs."

He was glad when they changed the subject because Mike was Deborah's ex-lover, the last man inside, and in this capacity he commanded shady loyalties. She must have liked him at one time, in fact she must have loved him because he was a bastard from any angle. Let her do her own condemning. *Tactics.*

"Thank you, that was marvelous."

"Marvelous," he said, and paid.

The worrying part of the evening was the discotheque. He wanted to cancel. They could put on her radio, dance at home. Over the dead coffee cups he said he had a very slight pain behind his eyes and he feared the flashing lights. She tapped the empty bottle of wine sardonically and then said "I'll go on my own." He couldn't let her do that although she probably would have enjoyed herself more reeling with hot men she had never met across the dance floor, rather than with Gary.

He hoped they wouldn't let him through the doors but the gangsters-in-dinner-jackets nodded him and his doxy in, and a cashier with a shaved head snatched Gary's money (implying that she had better things to do, she didn't have to do this).

Inside it was hot so that you could choose between reviving yourself expensively at the bar or dehydrating quietly to the sound of music. Gary had no trouble deciding and even managed to persuade Deborah to have a cocktail, which she sipped suspiciously through a straw. They couldn't hear what they were saying, of course, and Gary couldn't speak body language. She was swaying gently in time but he didn't encourage her by doing any swaying of his own, rooting himself instead as if to say Bad news, I've decided not to dance. But when he had finished his beer and Deborah's eyes were beginning to float down to the tight dancerly bottoms on the dance floor (he thought) he said "I think we ought to dance."

"What gives you that idea? Anyone would think this was a discotheque."

That was it, he would never take her to a place like this again. As he danced he thought—he was not a bad dancer and could dance and think more or less at the same time—he thought that a relationship could take a certain amount of awkwardness when it started but it should always contain the promise of a moment when the two parties would curl up collectively on a settee and be comfortable together. Wasn't it a fact that this promise was absent from his relations with Deborah? If this was so, who was deluding whom? It might seem she was onto a good thing with Gary, her new money-man, and Dermot (not quite sure where he fitted in). That would be the conventional view. On the other hand here was he flicking his fingers and wagging his legs with a clear conscience because he loved being with her, while she was a mess of conflicts. If she didn't like him any amount of free food and entertainment was no compensation to her. If she did like him she was ruining her evenings by keeping him at a distance.

"You can let go of me now," she said.

"What?"

"The song has finished."

"Sorry, I was thinking about something."

It was good to hold her when the song was slow, and so saddening when they reset the decibels at loud and she wanted to move back a step and dance in her own space. She looked pretty with her arms swinging.

11th

"Good news about Gerald."

"It could have been better."

"Or worse."

"What do you reckon he's doing?"

"It sounds like some kind of nervous breakdown."

"I could see it coming, in retrospect."

"You don't leave a job suddenly without a good explanation. There's a brick fallen out of his wall."

"You're always leaving jobs for no reason."

"I wouldn't leave if there was no reason. There are always underlying causes."

"How long are you going to stay in your present job?"

"This one could last a long time. I've had my time as a nomad and degenerate."

"What did you do last night?"

"Got drunk in the Three Stockbrokers."

Wasn't it good to have a *real* chat, again. Wasn't it the most pleasant thing?

Dermot and Gary were talking again and, it being Sunday, they had to decide on their leisure program for the day.

"Do we have to listen to hymns?"

"I used to sing this at Sunday school."

"Oh well in that case." In the old days Gary would have been a monk, that was Dermot's opinion. He would have started in a small way in a back-street monastery and then moved on to have his own see. He had the severe calm you

needed and Dermot often caught him listening to organ reci-
tals. Nor was he interested to distraction in women's bodies,
nothing at least that couldn't be sublimated into bell-ringing or
hard cloister-walking.

"I thought maybe swimming," Gary said.

"You used to say the kids in the pool got on your nerves. I
remember the fracas you had with a young Turk."

"He put his elbow in my face."

"You put one in his."

"His was the first elbow."

"It was an accident. He was only about eleven."

"I know. I apologized when I calmed down and offered to
buy him a Tizer. He thought I said tiger."

"I wonder if Gerald's camping out. Geraldine tells me he's
quite practical when he has a mind."

"I thought we'd already established that he'd lost his
mind."

"Just a tent, a sleeping bag, his wits, and a pen to write his
postcards."

"Do you think he'll write to anyone else?"

"I wouldn't imagine. People don't normally write unless
there's a chance of a letter back."

"On the other hand he may have met a rich American
widow at the National Gallery, a Guggenheim or a Texan prin-
cess."

"Geraldine says he looks so strong and silent in his uniform."

"Against the glamorous backdrop of the fine arts."

"We're talking about considerable pulling power."

The telephone rang and it was Dermot's mother. He had
been neglecting her, by his own admission. She told him to
come home and he hesitated because he wanted to find out
what Deborah was doing. However, his mother negotiated
skillfully, her use of silence particularly brilliant.

"We'll go swimming and then I have to visit my mother."

The pool was the jewel in the borough crown, along with
its meals-on-wheels, which were said to be exceptionally tasty.

The entrance hall had a large board with plastic push-in letters giving a list of rules. You were not allowed to "ride on the shoulders of other bathers" or "interfere with other bathers," in the past a matter of personal regret for Dermot. The distinctive muffled screams from the pool sounded, as ever, like murder. Light-reflecting puddles littered the changing room, where men and boys put their clothes away, worried about their bodies, or proud. Dermot dived in, Gary slithered. In fact Dermot could hardly swim and panicked when he was equidistant from the four poolsides where the water slapped. He made thrashing sprints and then trod the blue water or hugged the tiled edge and watched. Gary was like a seal gliding heavily just below the surface. The pool was quiet and he was not interfered with by splashers or dawdlers. Nobody tried to ride on his shoulders. As Dermot stood with his arms flattened on the side of the pool he scanned the wet limbs and the slicked costumes and feared that in years to come when he was short of breath, the years of this century having clicked over like miles on a dashboard (1999 2000 2001), he would still be coming there to watch the young women. He saw one now herding an escaping breast back into her ambitious beachwear.

Afterwards they sat in the cafeteria overlooking the pool. Soused in chlorine, the whites of their eyes were threaded with red.

"Haven't you got a comb?" Gary asked. His own hair was glinting and parted in a hundred parallel places by the teeth of his tortoiseshell comb.

"They pull your hair out. I want Deborah to have something to run her fingers through."

"I suppose it would save her having to talk to you."

"I used to have this theory that people kissed so they wouldn't have to talk to each other."

"I can't see that theory standing the test of time."

"As I say, I used to have it. In fact they kiss to show off their intimacy. *Look, watch my lips.* Prostitutes don't kiss their punters."

"They would if they were paid for it."

"I don't think they'd be happy doing it, though. I imagine they'd charge more than for the stuff below the waist."

"I would."

"Yeah, *I* would."

They thought about that for a while as they stared down at the pool. It was good exercise for the imagination.

Dermot had to take the underground to his mother's house south of the river. He bought a bottle of sherry in a passing off-license and traveled the ten stops opposite a tramp-like figure (he didn't like to say *tramp* because, honestly, you never knew) who eyed his liquor dreamily.

He had stopped believing this part of London was home; it was now simply the place where he was brought up. Nobody recognized him in the street. This was not so astonishing because they hadn't seen him before. The population swarmed from place to place, chasing work and better houses.

Frank came to the door. He was seventeen inches taller than when they last met a month earlier.

"Hello Frank."

"What's wrong with your eye?" He had forgotten about his eye.

"You're supposed to say Hello Dermot."

"You're too old to be getting into fights."

"I fell off a bus."

"When I'm your age I'll be taking taxis everywhere."

When Dermot was sixteen he didn't have a twenty-seven-year-old brother to kick around. He had to make do with his older sister who had now gone to live far away in Aberdeen, though probably not as a direct result of Dermot kicking her around. His father had died at a bad age for Dermot (and a bad age for his father) when they were still shouting at each other about everything. They couldn't sit in the same room without shouting at each other. When his father died without warning in his sleep they were into the second week of a major dispute about respect. They had haggled over how much was due, how little. It was Dermot's testosterone settling. At sixteen it did all his talking for him. He thought it was him but it was his hormones, it was juvenile dementia, he was not himself. Dermot decided that if he had a sixteen-year-old child he would arrange to be away on business as often as possible.

His mother was at the kitchen sink and she held her wet hands out in front of her as Dermot kissed her.

"Can't you get one of the boys to do that?" he asked. "You're looking well."

"Good. How are you? *Who* are you?"

"It's only four weeks. Some sons never visit their mothers."

"You used to come once a week."

"You don't want me hanging around, another mouth to feed."

Malcolm slouched into the kitchen, looking pleased to see Dermot. He was a dog.

"What's happened to your eye?" She dried her hands and held Dermot's head up to the light as if it was a gourd with an inscription. "I expect you to set an example. You never do."

"It was a fight about a woman."

"You're not the fighting type. What came over you?"

"We men, we don't walk away from our responsibility. Am I a Povey?"

"Silly," she said. "Always joking."

Dermot started to dry the familiar plates and ask the questions an oldest son asks. Temperamentally he was a youngest son. He had no feeling for clan leadership and no aptitude. His mother, in any case, was a Mother Courage. Seven children, and she an atheist.

"How is Sally?" he asked.

"She's found another oil man."

"What happened to the last?"

"He lost two fingers in some drilling machinery."

"To lose one finger may be regarded as a misfortune. How's Mary?" Once upon a time he had a leaning for soft dark Mary which amounted to desire. He used to like sitting by her on the sofa while they watched the television, hoping she would grow tired and rest her head on his shoulder. Now she had coarsened very slightly and he loved her more legally, with a brother's concern.

"She's been a bit depressed lately, so has Douglas."

He wasn't as interested in the boys. Boys were boys.

"How is Douglas?" Perhaps he should vary his questions.

"He's afraid he might get malaria. The last letter had a whole page on mosquitoes. Sherry, how kind." Dermot used to worry that his brothers and sisters would turn out to be more successful than himself, accountants and nightclub owners, TV weathermen. It still worried him. Douglas was a doctor, Sally was a geophysicist. Mary was a traffic warden but she might easily become a nightclub owner. The three young boys were dragging out their educations and living at home. Growing up when they did, their work expectations were lower than Dermot's had been at their age.

They unscrewed the sherry and Dermot went to fetch brother Duncan and brother Dick, unidentical twins. Duncan was lying on his bed asleep with a sly smile on his face. Dermot left him alone and went to Dick who had a big dumbbell in each hand.

"Watch this," he said.

"Amazing."

"I do that thirty times every morning."

"Amazing."

"Are you taking the piss?"

"No, I'm impressed. I've never done weight training."

"You have to breathe out when you're doing the lifting and in when you relax."

"You can't breathe anyhow, then."

"No. A lot of people think you can. What have you done to your eye?"

That was what he meant about explanations, about there being a lot of them to get through.

"I've smudged my mascara. Come and have a sherry."

"Men that pump iron don't drink sherry."

Soon all his brothers would be men and then they would have children who would in due course also become men, or women. It was obvious, but worth repeating. Douglas already had a son and a wife. Uncle Dermot.

Dick came and drank sherry in spite of his doubts and together the four Poveys sat in the small living room. For three spirited years they had been nine in this house. They had had to go without things because they were so many. Dermot sometimes couldn't get into the bathroom for weeks at a time. He shared a room with Douglas who used to low in his sleep and they had self-conscious arguments about the merits of art and science: Dermot graduated in English and was drifting from job to job while Douglas was fixing cataracts and preserving lives in the subcontinent, so you could say Douglas won the argument.

"Are they looking after you, mum?" Dermot asked.

"No, I'm looking after them. Frank, do you have to scratch. Frank's got a girlfriend."

Dick looked ashamed. In spite of his dumbbells Dick was a seventeen-year-old bachelor boy.

"What's she like, Frank?"

"Alright. I don't want any advice."

"Don't be so touchy, Frank," said his mother. "We're just taking an interest."

"I think she's an old dog actually. If you really want to know."

"Don't show off, Frank."

"What about you, Dick?" Dermot asked.

"Yeah. I think she's an old dog too."

"What do you know about it?"

"Stop it you two. Dick's doing very well at school. I'm very proud of him. Frank's not doing *quite* so well."

"He's a disaster," said Dick, sipping his sherry. Frank seemed to enjoy this description and almost smiled, which disheartened Dick. He went upstairs.

"The fence at the bottom of the garden has got to be repaired," his mother explained. She had a streak of gray in the middle of her hair and Dermot was reminded of badgers, much as he loved her.

"Get one of the boys to hammer in a few nails. Dick's good with his hands."

"Yes I've heard that," Frank said and this time he did smile, but Dermot and his mother did not indulge him.

"It's ridiculous, you can't afford it. If I had any money I'd buy you a fence."

"You'll never have any money," Frank said. He was getting on Dermot's nerves.

"Do you want an eye like mine?"

"No."

"Go and play with your trains."

"Don't speak to your brother like that, Dermot."

He sighed. "He should show more respect."

Gary was in the back garden staring up at the sky. There was a pale sun and in the air the smell of wet leaves. Gary was a keen listener to "Gardeners' Question Time." He loved the words they used. They made you interested in things like moss. When he lived with his parents Gary used to grow vegetables and sell them to his mother (*"More* beetroot! Super!") because they liked him to spend as much time as possible in the garden. But that was years ago and he hadn't had a rake in his hand since. Now, sacrificing a quiet afternoon, he had suggested to Geraldine that he tidy up the back garden. She was with Gwen, whose husband was still at sea and was due to remain there. Gwen said "And you can do mine while you're out there," a rare piece of raillery. Geraldine didn't seem sure she wanted Gary loose on her leaves, not because he would do any damage (How do you damage a wilderness? You can't damage a wilderness.) but because it suggested her husband would not be back for a long while, if ever. He read this in her sudden melancholy.

But Gary wanted to help and it was bad for her to dwell on the past, as conventional wisdom so rightly had it.

He'd never been inside Gerald's shed before and as he turned the key Gary feared it might hold a clue to his departure, the evidence of an unsociable predilection that had driven him away, a stack of dead young men or elderly women, an alembic containing an evil froth. In fact there was a rake and not much more. It was surprising that Gerald didn't potter more down here and brood on existence in this little house with one window.

A tree in the corner of the garden was responsible for the oily leaves, and there was another in Gwen's garden which had contributed. Gary didn't know trees too well—it was in the nature of radio programs to leave you in the dark to some extent. Now, anyway, these two larches or oaks or whatever were empty although they did hold in their branches dark clots that must be nests. In the summer Gary woke up to the sound of birds. He didn't know what types of bird they were either. They were not pigeons. Gary had an uneasy feeling about nature. It was enormously complicated, of course. He had heard that even the people who know the most about nature knew almost nothing, in fact they were discovering things they didn't understand day in day out. The storehouse of knowledge was a mere shed, a cardboard box, compared with the warehouse of ignorance, if you could believe that.

Properly humble, Gary raked his leaves.

The other house next door had been up for sale for months and was empty. Its garden was a disgrace to the neighborhood which, in its turn, some considered a disgrace. The garden was landscaped with rubbish from neighbors, donations of sacks of rubble, old iron, a mirror cracked from side to side. Gary himself had not given anything but it was on the record that, generally speaking, he was a litterer. It was a habit he couldn't break and it didn't bring him sympathy like some addictions do. It had started harmlessly enough with a sweet paper, perhaps, on the way home from school, but led to crisp packets and before long newspapers, which he fed whole to the gutters and pavements. He hated having garbage in his pockets and in his hands, it was no more complicated than that. It made him feel untidy. But on the rare occasions he visited the countryside he found littering impossible. He could only defile concrete and this suggested to Gary that he should be living in the country, but he hated the country.

He swept the leaves into six piles and then merged the six into three. Geraldine appeared at the ground floor window, pulling back the net curtains, waving encouragement. He merged the three piles into one, after some thought. As he decided what to do with this one pile he heard noises behind one of the windows, shouts wrapped in glass and masonry. They were coming from Deborah's room under the eaves. Gary had never heard her raise her cool voice but he supposed this was what it would sound like when she got angry and threw it from the top of a house. The man was Mike, unless she knew other men with grit in their voices.

He walked through Geraldine's kitchen, still carrying the rake and on its prongs a number of spitted leaves. He hesitated in front of Geraldine and Gwen.

"Have you just let a man in?"

"You're leaving dirt on the carpet," Gwen said.

"It's a friend of Deborah's," Geraldine said.

Gary was tempted to sit down and drink tea with the ladies. He had no wish to expose himself to unnecessary risks by going upstairs.

"Is there some problem?" Geraldine asked.

"I can see at least ten footmarks," Gwen said.

"Deborah's friend is a hoodlum. I've told you about him." He wished he had been more explicit. He should have posted a warning notice on the pink door. "He's not even her friend."

"Shall I call the police?" Geraldine wanted to know.

"The police?" he shouted. "Whatever for, the police?" He had no reason to shout at her like this. Realizing he would have to go upstairs, he banged the handle of the rake on the floor and leaves and leaf mold fell about the room.

"You're dropping leaves on the carpet."

"Shut up Gwen," he said.

Upstairs, voices were still raised. He paused outside her door. She was saying No No No while he seemed to be moving among her furniture as he talked tough in his harsh inflexible voice. It could be argued, Gary argued, that they were better left settling their differences on their own, but the likelihood was small that she had invited him over. He had invited himself over and if he did not get satisfaction (Gary hoped he would not, in a way. It sounded like he wasn't getting it.) he would probably settle their differences by throwing her down the stairs. Gary remembered the slanging that had gone on some days before between Geraldine and Gerald of blessed memory. The house was becoming argumentative.

Gary still had his rake in his hand and was wearing Dermot's yellow rubber boots which were left over from a job he once had in a turkey insemination factory. Should he go and slip into something less intrusive? No, there was no time. Deborah had begun to yelp.

"Get the fuck out," Mike said. He seemed frustrated to see Gary.

"Deborah, shall I leave?"

"No." She stood with her back to the wall, her arms crossed high on her chest. Mike stood close to her and Gary noted abstractly that he had had his hair cut.

"I heard you shouting from the garden," he explained.

"I'm trying to *talk* here," he shouted.

"Go away will you. I've nothing else to say," she said.

Gary sensed that if he wasn't there Mike might at this point have tried to appeal to her sympathy. He could hardly do that now with Gary standing there in his yellow boots. That was why he resented Gary being there, preventing him from using all his persuasions. (All men had heard that women liked them to appear vulnerable some of the time. It suited him fine because that was how they felt almost *all* of the time.)

"We've been through this before," Gary said.

"Will you *leave*," he answered, and kicked over a chair. "This is a private interview."

"So how come I could hear you in the garden?"

"Because you're fucking nosy. You fancy her, is that it?"

What should he say? He wanted to say yes.

"That's got nothing to do with it."

There was a long pause. Gary wanted to know why Deborah was saying nothing. Somebody say something.

"If you don't leave soon Mike I'm going to call the police," she said. Gary couldn't understand why he'd stopped Geraldine calling them. They were there to be called. They probably *liked* getting calls.

"Don't be stupid."

"I'm going to do that every time you turn up here." She didn't actually have a telephone but Mike could not have known. Gary had the impression from a new tautness in his posture that Mike had done with talking, that his frustration was now too big a thing for that.

He moved towards Gary, who arranged the wire prongs of his rake at a hawkish angle and stepped back on the bridge of Geraldine's foot.

"Sorry."

"I just came up to say hello," she said, the trace of a wince, looking through at the alleged hoodlum. In the days before Gerald's disappearance, when she was so very alive, she would have whisked Mike down to her kitchen and made him wind wool or tell her about himself. "This is Gwen."

"Good afternoon," Gwen said, craning round the door.

"I don't think I caught your name?"

"Michael," he said uneasily.

"Gwen's husband is called Michael," Geraldine went on. "He's in—where is it he is, Gwen?"

"Singapore," she dropped drily, craning her head again to be heard.

"I have to go." He walked towards the door where Geraldine stood, dressed in roses, and as he passed Gary he stopped, lifted his finger threateningly in his face and said between his teeth "Soon."

"He's so melodramatic," Gary said.

Deborah had gone when Dermot arrived home. It was inevitable that she should have friends to visit and places to be seen in but he hurt from not knowing where she was. He'd left his mother prematurely, at the sink where he had found her, which was no kind of behavior for a son who claimed to care. Dermot didn't collect friends because, like possessions, they needed constant looking after. Gary was even worse and had dragged him down (he hoped his personality wasn't being destroyed systematically, he wouldn't have liked that). Other people such as Deborah might have seven or eight close friends assembled over the years but Dermot only had ex-lovers whom he would have liked to see more often even if it was he who caused their separation as he often had. He liked the company of women he had slept with—he wasn't sure if it was because carnal knowledge increased the sexual forces or dissolved them. They, in any case, weren't as keen to see him after they for one reason or another had parted, even when they had both promised to keep in touch.

But what, incidentally, was all this talk about Dermot sleeping around, Dermot-despoiler-corrupter? It was Gary's talk. Dermot couldn't remember how many lovers he had had but he could work it out if he sat down with a pencil. There probably weren't so many. There was a query against his stamina, yes. After a month or two dissatisfactions often surfaced which he was not prepared to ride out—how did you *work at* a relationship, for example? It sounded like a contradiction in terms. Either you had one or you didn't—but this, he felt, was because he found it easy to talk to women he could understand and he didn't love women he could understand so easily, so quickly. They probably felt the same.

As for men, Dermot preferred women. He would never have what he considered a proper friendship with a man, although he didn't mind talking to them.

"And then," Gary said, "we all had a good laugh about it."

Dermot couldn't imagine Gwen laughing, her head thrown back. Gary had a giggle which he kept for odd moments but otherwise he was not a laugher. Deborah seldom even smiled and Geraldine had given it up since Gerald went missing. Dermot didn't actually believe *one* of them had had a good laugh about it.

"I'm glad to see she's held out," he said.

"I think that'll be his last visit. If it was me I'd move on to someone else."

"Poor Mike. He's got it bad."

"What a fool he's making of himself."

12th

The day glowed bright behind Gary's bedroom curtains and he heard a knocking on the edge of his consciousness. It was unusual for him to sleep through a winter sunrise.

He went to the door expecting it to be Geraldine.

"Morning Geraldine."

"Another postcard," she said. Today she was wearing a dress with small blue flowers. Gary was training himself to notice what women wore.

"Who's it from?"

"Gerald, Gerald, who else." She was badly agitated.

"I'm sorry. I'm half asleep."

She put it into his hand. There were four views of Brighton—The Dolphinarium, Sea Front, Royal Pavillion and, more incongruously, a couple coming out of a fish-and-chip shop. On the reverse side the Queen had again lost a lot of her cheek and this time all of her nose under the words *South Coast*. The little handwriting there was was if anything more elegant than before—it would in a sense have been more encouraging if it was showing signs of collapse. The card was addressed to Geraldine, its message

Thinking of you. It's blustery down here.

"He's becoming prolific," he said.

"It looks like he's in Brighton."

"You're right."

"I want you to go down and look for him. You don't go to work on Mondays."

"Why don't you go?"

"*You think I don't want to go?*" she screamed. She calmed down, running a hand over her forehead.

"I'm still half asleep," he explained doggedly. "Of course I'll go."

"I can't walk very far, you see, and you'll have to try the guest houses and hotels and just walk the streets until you find him."

She had a bad knee.

"You stay and wait by the telephone," he said, to encourage her and make up for his earlier reluctance. He'd never been to Brighton before. He didn't get around as much as he should.

"I feel so excited," she said. "Soon it will all be over."

"You say he was wearing a green anorak and brown trousers?"

"And black shoes."

"Black shoes with brown trousers?"

"But he may have bought some new clothes, of course, although as a rule he hated clothes shops."

Hated, she had said.

"*Hates,*" he corrected and she looked at him without understanding.

He got dressed into his most forgiving walking shoes and as he was about to leave the telephone rang. It was the bed people.

"We have your bed," the gentleman said, as if it was an abduction.

"Ah, my new bed. I'd forgotten."

"We have it."

"Well can *I* have it please?"

"When will you be in?"

"Normally I'm in on Monday but today I'm not in."

"It says here Monday is the most convenient day."

"But I have to go to Brighton." He couldn't bother Geral-

133

dine, who was on edge, but Dermot had the next day off. "How about tomorrow morning?"

"It says on the form Monday is the most convenient day."

"Look, *forget Monday.* If you like you can cross out Monday and write in Tuesday above. How would that be?"

"I can't tamper with a form. What time tomorrow?"

"As early as possible."

"So that's Tuesday morning, not Monday. Have a nice day in Bournemouth."

"Brighton."

Gary had mixed feelings about visiting the south coast on a Monday in November. There was a strong suggestion of dampness and decay about these places when the last brown body had left the promenade and before the Christmas lights began to drape themselves all over. The rain was a spray shafting in from the sea, or so it went in Southend which he used to visit with his parents at the end of the season, when even the paint on the beach huts had started to come away. On the other hand looking for Gerald was a good deed and the weather might turn out fine. The bed was an annoyance but he had gone without it this long, and this way he was getting two days' anticipation for the price of one.

Victoria Station had a bleary look and its thick cavernous voice, echoing down from the rafters, still managed to sound tart. "Will the person cycling on the concourse please stop immediately." Gary looked up expecting to see glowering eyes set into the roof and smoke-blackened lips thin with scorn.

He bought his ticket by shouting through the latticed porthole and walked to the bookstall, a phosphorescent chalet where travelers were killing time. His hand hovered over the newspapers but the tabloids looked dingy and the broadsheets were depressing. He watched the departures and arrivals board flutter, erasing whole communities. It fluttered again, restoring prosperous dormitories and southern bolt-holes in series all the way down to the sea or stopping short before tarmac became fields in Surrey and Kent.

The other people rushed or they stood still. The ones that

rushed often carried sharp-cornered bags which gave their dash through the stationary crowd a risky flavor. Gary made a slow tour of the twin hangars while he waited for his train. His attention was arrested by the electric, honking vehicle that carried luggage in lazy loops of its snaking carriages.

He walked to the front of the long train, but not the very front where he would get killed if the land had slipped or if the signals were doolally. Although he had planned to look out of the window he fell asleep, as far as he remembered, when the train thundered hollowly across the Thames.

He bought a map of Brighton and picked up a free list of hotels, guesthouses, hostels, campsites.

"Good morning, do you have anyone staying here by the name of Gerald Jones?"

"I don't believe I do. May I ask why?"

"He's gone missing. Never mind."

"No, don't go, I'm interested."

Gary talked to his first bored receptionist of the day, a bright young man behind a polished desk. They theorized on temporary madness. Gary pointed out that Gerald was no longer totally missing. *Absent* was a better description. His postcards were desperate signposts, was the conclusion they reached. He was not sending reassurance, he was sending them in order to bring help without actually asking for it. It was possible, naturally, he had already moved on to Littlehampton or Worthing, bad places to be in November if you are at all under the weather.

"You should have brought a photograph with you to show people."

"You don't think that would be going too far?"

Gary couldn't help thinking, as they discussed sleuthing methodology, that he would excel at hotel receptionry. It was a myth that you had to be polite. You had to be firm. Nobody liked to be called Sir or Madam any more and they preferred to carry their own bags because money was tight, so that was okay.

"*Walkabout*, they call it in Australia," he was saying.

"I've heard that word."

135

"When an aborigine goes off for a few days out of some atavistic need."

"I don't think Gerald has ancestors in Brighton, he's more Swansea. But he used to come here when he was just married so you may have something. I don't know if we can really equate the seafront and the outback."

Gary left and trailed round a dozen or more establishments, most of which were helpful, some overtly suspicious.

"Are you police?"

"No. I'm just looking for this man."

"Private detective?"

"Nothing like that."

"What's he done? There's nobody peculiar or violent here."

"I just need to locate him. He's not peculiar or violent."

"He's not here."

"Can I see your hotel register?"

"You most certainly can not."

"You bastard."

These wet and windy towns. What Gary liked about London—and you didn't get this in many places—was that you could walk all day without running out of town, whereas here you could only walk so long before there was a petering out. According to the book he stopped to read in a bookshop (holding the book barely open to preserve its spine for the genuine purchaser—he could be considerate) Brighton swelled to twice its size in the summer, a fascinating statistic.

Walking everywhere, he saw a lot of hotel foyers. They had bells that you pressed to gain the attention of uniformed personnel. Before not so long he got tired of asking the same questions and became convinced Gerald was in Littlehampton. He went into a fish restaurant because this was the seaside, although he realized that the fish they served were probably caught on the other side of the world and brought over in a refrigerated ship two miles long. On the table there was an especially large plastic tomato and the waitress appeared to be Greek, reminding him of London.

"A huge piece of cod, please. No, no. Make that a *vast* piece."

The rest of the afternoon he spent hanging around in populous areas looking out for Gerald's square face and trying to walk off the effects of the fish, which had indeed been bulky. He had no clear picture in his mind of what the back of Gerald's head looked like and had to circle a number of men to eliminate their faces from the search. Finally his feet grew hot and his knees tired. He thought of Geraldine sitting by the telephone and had to feel sorry. It wasn't easy for him to put himself in her position or anybody's position, even Dermot's. There was no equivalent of Gerald in Gary's life. Admittedly, it would have been a shock to lose, just to lose, his mother or father, George or Dermot. He would have come to Brighton to look for any of these four but the difficulty would have arisen if they had written from a less accessible coastline. How far exactly was he prepared to travel on someone else's behalf or behest? Only so far. His commitment to his father would be in the balance as early as Lowestoft.

It grew dark and Gary had one last look among the pedestrians who were trotting now in the rush hour. They had a rush hour down here as well, but it didn't fret and fume as much as London's big chaos. There the traffic lay in snakes of dead metal but here it never stopped slithering. The quality of life was higher in the provinces but Gary wanted to live and die in London, particularly to live. He thrived on irrational choices.

Gerald was not there. What a tease *he* was turning out to be.

"You said you'd have it in last Thursday."

"Did we actually say that?"

"Last Thursday."

"What day is it today?" Dermot asked.

"Monday."

"And we said last Thursday?"

"Yes."

"Ah." Who were the most dangerous complainers—men who looked like lawyers? Dermot thought so. "We were overoptimistic. May I apologize on behalf of everyone."

"What good will that do?"

"No good, obviously. Mind you, neither will your complaining do any good, I'm afraid." Dermot didn't like this man, which entitled him to be indelicate. He had a harder time with customers with whom he sympathized, who were entitled to finely spun explanations. "I expect you've come out of your way to get this book."

"Fortunately I was passing."

"Now I don't feel so bad."

"Will you put one aside for me when they come in?"

Alas, he was turning out to be a little darling. Dermot did feel bad; here was this poor man, trying to buy a book.

"I promise I will. I'll see to it personally."

"Many thanks."

"Many many thanks."

You could grow to hate books, working in a book department. Or, worse than that, people could begin to irritate you. Dermot was irritated by anyone who hung around the shelves reading for hours on end. They did that. They picked up a novel or an autobiography and stood, rocking back on their heels or with their weight comfortably on one foot, for minutes or hours, flicking backwards and forwards or turning the pages tirelessly one by one. Dermot was *furious* that this irritated him because God knows why shouldn't they, it didn't make his life any the poorer. But that was the point about irritation, that its causes were so annoyingly trivial. Gary used to upset him by stroking his beard and this he found more upsetting than plane crashes and Middle Eastern wars.

Shortly after Dermot had got on the bus to go home a woman climbed onto the upper deck and started to sing. It was happening more and more in London. The conductor, Dermot noticed, didn't try to sell her a ticket for fear of provoking colorful acts of madness and Dermot stored this knowledge for the time when he became very poor.

Gary was jangling his keys at the door when Dermot drew up.

"I've just been to Brighton," he said, finding the key.

"What a nice idea."

"I didn't want to go. It was Gerald."

"He's there, is he?"

"Doesn't seem to be."

He knocked on Geraldine's door and they both went on in. She was sitting by the telephone, as they had agreed.

"I must have gone to every hotel."

She was badly drawn, as if the person who normally cartooned her face was away on holiday. "I'm sure he's there."

"He probably can't afford a hotel," Dermot said. "Under the pier is traditional."

"I looked. You think I would have forgotten to look there?" Why hadn't he thought of looking under the pier? A mistake. "Of course, he may creep back at nightfall."

"I can't bear to do nothing. I've had a terrible afternoon," she said quietly.

"Dermot can go and look tomorrow."

"You said you looked everywhere," he said.

"But not at the same time," Gary snapped. "I may have been looking under the pier when he was sitting in the bus station, and been looking in the bus station when he had moved on to that awful Pavillion. I'm not simultaneous."

"Please go, Dermot."

"You know Geraldine can't walk far with her leg."

"I *want* to go." He had planned to go to the launderette because he was down to odd socks. He had a lot of these and didn't like to throw them away because the more odd socks he acquired the less odd they became (when he only had two they were completely odd, one gray and one green, but now he could combine green with green and gray with gray, although not precisely the same shade or texture). Also he needed to take his suit into the instant dry cleaners before it got so foul it started to attack its buttons, corrode its lining. He had been nurturing a scheme to take a forest of red roses to Deborah at work, but he was going to Brighton instead.

"He sent another postcard, you see," she explained from

her seat by the white telephone, "of Brighton."

"I know it quite well. I had a girlfriend there one summer. The fares were crippling."

"I'll pay for you to go," she said.

"No I didn't mean that. It was just an autobiographical footnote."

"And don't think we don't appreciate it," Gary said. "We like the personal angle, don't we, Geraldine?"

"He could have moved on," she frowned, "but why then would he have sent a postcard?"

"Of course."

It occurred to Gary only now that if he had found Gerald he would not have known what to do. He would have put his case: your wife is worried sick; we are all worried sick; you will lose your job if you have not lost it already. But Gerald may have been happy by the sea in spite of the postcards and have folded his arms and refused to go with Gary to the station. He may have found him hand in hand with a young and attractive woman, in which case there would be an awkward discussion, possibly even a *scene*. It would not have been possible to call a policeman and have Gerald crated up and returned to his anxious spouse, because he was not underage or dangerous, although they might use mental instability as leverage. Perhaps it was just as well Gary hadn't found Gerald, because that would not have been the end of the story, it would have been the beginning.

"Dermot, make Geraldine a cup of tea."

"I'm afraid the leaves have blown all over the garden again," she said, turning to Gary as Dermot went into the kitchen. "I've been listening to them rustle all day."

"You should be doing something more active than listening to leaves rustle."

"Sorry."

"I don't mean to be harsh but this place needs dusting."

"I can't concentrate on anything."

"Dusting doesn't take much concentration, Geraldine. I'd say that was a pretty poor excuse. As I say, the last thing I mean is to be harsh."

"I don't *care* if it's dirty in here," she cried. "The dust doesn't matter," she half wailed, half said.

"Leave Geraldine alone," Dermot shouted from the next room.

Gary wasn't happy to hear Dermot shouting what he considered unhelpful and ingratiating remarks. Dermot always took the soft line, regardless of whether the hard line was the better instrument of the two. Gary didn't want to offend Geraldine, he wanted to reactivate her.

"I'm just trying to make you fight a little," he told her.

"Is it because you're cross about the leaves?"

"It's got nothing to do with the leaves." It was not as though antagonism was the most avant-garde trick in the psychotherapist's casebook. Anyhow, she had allowed herself to be offended by his robust approach so he retreated behind the soft line. "You're right, the dust doesn't matter. As Dermot will tell you, I'm obsessional, that's all. You are quite correct to think of Gerald first and housework second. Distant second."

"Gary has a point," Dermot said, changing his mind. "It does no good just sitting around. You've got to carry on as if nothing had happened. Do you like your milk in before the tea or after?"

"As it comes."

"I can do either. It's absolutely no problem."

"Dermot, she said as it comes."

Gary's legs were already stiff from walking, his shins in particular had brittle steel implants, his calves were lead.

"What does the back of Gerald's head look like, Geraldine?" Gary asked, and made her cry. (What were these triggers that set her weeping? Was it the conjunction of their two names in one sentence or the picture of the back of her husband's head or had these tears been in the air for some time?)

"I can't remember," she said through her tears. "I actually can't."

"Don't cry," Dermot said.

"No, don't cry."

They both knew that crying was a good idea and a source

of great release but *don't cry* was something you said.

"I want to," she said through her hands.

"Okay."

"You go ahead then."

"You will find him tomorrow, won't you, Dermot?" she wept.

"Sure."

Something kept Dermot away from Deborah that night. She was upstairs because he could hear her light tread above his head. There were times when you didn't want to see the woman you love, or the man you love if it is a man. Take Dermot. If he felt he was bad company for any reason he liked to stay at home or drink incognito. It was a form of self-censorship he didn't often use because he considered himself amusing company and no mistake, most of the time. And at other times, like tonight, he just didn't want to see the one person who he had to watch so very carefully, the loved one. There was so much tension in the company of the woman who claimed his whole attention. Deborah deserved her evening off and she might even wonder what was up with those boys, not coming to see her all of a sudden. She might be up there thinking *What have I done?* He had a favorite scenario, a steamy fancy, in which she was upstairs spraying musk on the insides of her thighs and saying to herself *Where is Dermot, doesn't he love me anymore?*

Gary was sitting in the kitchen turning over the blue-backed playing cards. He decided that if this game of patience came out successfully he would go up and see Deborah. It did not. Undeterred, he made the same deal a second time. He was more than beaten this time, he was humiliated by the cards. There was a small element of skill in this game, only a pittance in fact, but Gary sweated and hypothesized over the turn of each card. When he was engaged by some activity or spectacle his lips always fell apart and occasionally the tip of his tongue could be seen hovering in the lobby of his mouth. This was one of these occasions. He could have gone up to see her without this lottery because she was upstairs alright. He had turned the radio off in order to hear the soles of her feet on the ceiling. There was a floorboard near her door which squealed, and a hint of taped music in the background. He wanted to go to her but Dermot seemed to be watching him and challenging him to make a fool of himself by creeping to her door like an old butler. So reluctantly he gave up the cards and turned the radio back on. For a change he listened to the police fighting crime on a lonely airwave. Their language was an odd garble and for this reason they reminded him of disc jockeys, jockeying order into the affairs of the capital. It was eerie listening, this talk of lemurs, tangos and proceeding to disturbances, and after a while Gary walked to his bedroom and rearranged his furniture to make way for the arrival tomorrow of his big bed.

13th

"What did you do this weekend, George?"

"I put up some shelves."

"You must have shelves all over your house by now. They're a feature of our reviews of the weekend."

"Not all over."

"I wouldn't be surprised if you had shelves on the outside of your house."

"No, they're all inside."

"Are they your wife's idea or do you enjoy putting them up?"

"It's hard to say. We agree on almost everything."

"That's unusual."

"Not for us. How was your weekend, Gary?"

"Crowded."

"You had people round did you?"

"Crowded with incident. We never have people round." He had always wanted to lead a busy life because in spite of himself he was impressed by fast living.

"What kind of incident was that?"

"I was at a discotheque until three o'clock on Saturday night."

"Well."

"I know."

"Actually, isn't that a normal sort of time for a discotheque?"

"Oh yes." Gary was also impressed by people who stayed out late. He liked to tell people whenever he was still up after

144

about one o'clock. It was almost certainly linked to his parents' insistence, when he was young, that he be in bed at least two hours before other boys of the same age. They were lax about everything else apart from this curfew which meant that Gary spent at least half of the first twelve years of his life in pajamas. At the time, although he protested, he interpreted this as overprotection, a product of their love. He now believed they simply wanted him out of the way so they could smoke cigarettes in front of the television, conjugate their love on the kitchen table or stairs and basically do what they wanted to do without him watching from a corner.

"How are you getting on with that girl of yours?"

"I can't tell."

"You should be able to by now. My wife was giving me signals as soon as she met me."

"I've only known her about ten days."

"How much did Saturday night cost you?"

"I've no idea. At least two hundred pounds."

"You can't do that every Saturday can you."

"Maybe not."

He was right. George talked sense. Deborah hadn't been giving any signals.

"Shall I bring it up then?"

"Please. Have you got a mate?"

"I've got mates, yes," he said, and was gone.

Dermot had been a driver's mate for a while. He had to talk to the driver. That was the job. Dermot would sit with his feet on the dashboard and make comments that he thought were expected of him (cyclists, woman drivers, football), and then once in a while they jumped out and delivered a piece of ugly furniture.

The bed came wrapped in a thick plastic sheet which allowed the two shifters the luxury of resting it on the damp pavement as they went back to shut the van door.

"Is this for you, then?" the driver shouted to him.

"No, I already have one thank you."

"You have to assemble it yourself," he explained as he

staggered past Dermot with his half of the base of the bed.

"I should just prop it against the wall," Dermot said when they were upstairs. "I'm in a bit of a hurry, unfortunately."

"Why, have you got to go to Bournemouth like the other chap."

"Brighton, yes."

They brought the mattress and the other bits and Dermot signed in Gary's name because it made a change from his own signature, which he had written a thousand times.

"You must come round to my house one of these days, Gary."

"If you're sure your wife wouldn't mind."

"She likes having people to eat. Is there anything you don't like in the way of food?"

"Celery."

"Let me make a note of that before I forget." Gary couldn't see George, unless he put his head round the partition, but he vividly imagined him writing *celery* on the back of an old envelope.

"You haven't been over to my place either, George. You and Marjorie are very welcome."

"She's not too keen on coming down to London, that's the problem. She says it's smelly and loud and there are too many tall buildings."

"All perfectly valid points."

"Was there anything other than celery?"

"No, celery's the only thing."

Perhaps he should have refused this invitation which bridged two worlds in a small but dangerous way. On the other hand it might be a charming evening.

"Our flat's nothing special," Gary said, to make George feel less guilty about turning down a perfectly good return invitation.

"When we drive down to Rugby she makes me drive around London. Skirt it, I mean. I've told her it adds half an hour to our journey."

"Never mind. You can come to dinner if I ever move out to the country."

"I look forward to that, Gary."

♦ ♦ ♦

Dermot stood with his arms on the balustrade and stared out over the undulating pebble beach which looked like cobbled waves. The sea was gray and empty of ships. It rolled elegantly towards Dermot but then stopped at the foothills of the shingle, depriving him of that crackling-hissing sound of the high tide trying to suck the smooth stones into the sea.

He turned away and walked past the hotels facing the sea and into the shopping center. Green anorak, brown trousers, black shoes. Possibly. Geraldine never had described the back of his head, perhaps she really had forgotten. Dermot himself was wearing a blue donkey jacket with neon shoulders, the physical remains of a job he once had as a roadmender. It was one of his most arduous jobs, the more so because the road was the M1. They were taken in coaches at dawn and brought back at dusk. After that job Dermot had gone clerical, saying he would no longer labor. He was wearing the jacket today because he thought the tangerine epaulets would attract Gerald, although there was a good chance they would repel him.

On the train down he had been thinking about Deborah and regretting not visiting her the day before. He hadn't seen her for days and she might be one of those people who need constant reminding that they are loved obsessively. In spite of her composed looks her life could not be easy and it must be difficult to keep pumping out composure when the man she lived with so recently continued to love her with such loathing. Dermot made the decision between Haywards Heath and Burgess Hill that he wanted to live with Deborah. It was less a decision than a confirmation and was only robbed of meaning by the fact that she would not want to live with him. It was as if he had decided he wanted to be five foot eleven rather than five foot eight or confirmed his desire, between Haywards Heath and Burgess Hill, to live to a very old age. And yet he had not had an idea like this for five or six years. This was a good reason to take it seriously—nowadays he got the same old thoughts all the time, recycled ideas. For all these years he had been happy to live apart from his girls. Not now.

Dermot had no system, he just wandered. Nothing much had changed since the summer he commuted regularly to see Alison who attended deck chairs by day and lay with him by night. She was beautifully brown but always complaining of tired legs, and sure enough they did dangle a shade limply either side of Dermot's vigorous pumping thighs as they did their lying dance. Walking on the beach all day, she said, was like treading grapes for eight hours and the clatter of stones applauding each step soon drove her to despair.

Was that Gerald? Was that his shape over there walking slowly by the supermarket, the café, the kiosk? Dermot started to run towards the figure but people stopped to look at him so he reverted to a wild and leggy walk. Then he lost the green shoulders from view and began to run again in his roadmender's fancy dress, dodging the flower troughs, the prams and people. Gerald was not where he had been. Dermot rode the escalators down to the lower floor, hanging over the side and peering into the underworld where a few underprivileged shops, set in stone, glowered on the fringe of the subterranean car park. Dermot, who didn't swear, said *shit* and *shhitt* when he found nobody downstairs. He took the escalators back up, running so fast up the metal stairs that their combined speeds fired him off the other end onto his knees and hands.

Gerald was one of the people watching him dust the shopping center off his jeans.

"Gerald. I've been looking for you."

"Me?"

While he had been away Gerald had not got a taste for wordy rejoinders. He looked more bullish than before and even less responsive.

"Come and talk to me."

"Why?"

Dermot was not happy in this role. He had never been a persuasive person.

"We received your two postcards."

"Good."

148

"Gerald, what are you doing down here?"

"I had to get away."

"You're killing your wife."

"I'm sorry."

"You don't sound sorry."

Dermot eased him in the direction of the café, which gave him time to think about what to say and to admire Gerald's brightly polished shoes. If he was sleeping under the pier he must be sleeping with shoeshine boys.

"Have you had lunch?"

"Yes."

Dermot didn't have very much money left in his pay packet. He was trying to live within his means but the temptation was to burst out of them and live outside. Not buying food seemed as good a way as any to save money.

"So have I. How about coffee?"

"I'll have a glass of orange squash."

Sliding the tray along its track Dermot felt like a parent with a delinquent child. Gerald followed him down the self-service alley looking through the scratched plastic at the trifles.

"Are you sure you don't want anything?"

"I've got money, Dermot."

"That's all right then." It was encouraging to hear Gerald say his name. He was always flattered when people took the trouble to tell him who he was.

The orange squash came in a tall glass which felt unstable on the tray next to Dermot's short coffee. The walls were hung with Aztec motifs in lumpy fiberglass and people sat in corners reading the *Evening Argus*.

"Shall we sit here?"

"It doesn't matter."

They did sit there in the window, where they could watch the shoppers trekking across the stained slabs with their plastic bags, adding bags as they went.

"First of all," Dermot said, "what are you living on?"

"I've always had money put by."

"What for?"

149

"To treat Geraldine, maybe. A holiday."

"But you decided to take it on your own."

"This isn't a holiday."

"Nor is it for her."

"It's nothing to do with her."

"Are you coming home?" he asked after a pause.

"I don't know."

"You must come."

"There is no must."

"How long have you been married?"

"A long time."

"Gerald, I can't cope with this. You're having a nervous breakdown, or something. It's ridiculous me talking to you here."

"I know."

"When what you need is specialized help."

"No."

He didn't want to frighten Gerald by probing but he had to ask questions. It was probably a mistake to mention nervous breakdowns when he had no idea if that was what it was. What did a nervous breakdown look like? He had heard that one characteristic was that the patient found very small things *incredibly* worrying. Gerald wasn't showing any of these symptoms.

"You're just depressed. Why don't you come home and think about it there, see a doctor."

"There's nothing wrong with me."

"Okay, I won't make you see a doctor."

"I'm fine."

"So why did you leave so suddenly?"

"I didn't want to have to explain."

"Don't you think that indicates something is wrong?"

"No."

He scratched his chin aimlessly. Now Dermot thought about it, Gerald didn't look so unhappy. He seemed calm and sure of himself.

"Where are you staying?"

"I've rented a room."

"What's the address?"

"I don't want to tell you."

"Give me a clue."

"It overlooks the sea."

A young couple walked past outside holding hands and swinging them playfully. Dermot decided it was time to broaden the conversation to show that there were other things going on. It was to put Gerald in his place that he said "I've fallen in love with your new lodger."

"I remember her." There was a flicker of interest in his eyes.

"She's beautiful. Gerald," he asked, remembering another question from his list of questions, "where was it you used to disappear to after work?"

"I went for a drink with my colleagues," he said, losing his calm.

"No you didn't."

"Yes I did."

"I won't tell Geraldine if that's what you want."

"I went to paint."

"Paint what?"

"Painting classes. I was enrolled."

"So what was the big secret?"

"There was no big secret."

Dermot had not noticed before but he noticed it now. There was a black fleck of paint on Gerald's otherwise pale gray temple.

"Have you come down here to paint?"

"I may do a little."

"Why can't you do it in London?"

"You're asking too many questions."

"We'll have a break. Let me get you an orange squash."

"No, I'll have coffee this time."

He was gone, of course, when Dermot got back. Asking for a coffee had been a neat touch for a man with a question mark against his mental health. It had lulled Dermot into thinking Gerald wanted to stay and give him the full version.

For a moment Dermot stood with the tray in his hands,

assuming that he was about to put it down and run after him. But as the seconds ticked by he realized that this was not going to happen so he sat down and drank his coffee quietly.

How do the Swedes do it? Don't the Finns want to put a stake through their own hearts? Winter darkness. Apparently in deep winter they had so few daylight minutes in those parts that it wasn't worth pulling back the curtains. Gary came over gloomy when darkness fell as late as half past four.

"Just look at that."

"What?"

"Just look at it, George. All that darkness."

"You should go to Scandinavia."

"I was just thinking about them."

"They have the midnight sun over there."

"That's only in the summer."

"I suppose so."

"They don't tell you about the dark noons in winter."

"You know why it happens, of course. It's so that we get a balanced diet. If the weather was the same all the year round, so would the vegetation be. Either we'd be eating tomatoes all the year round, or cabbages."

"Are you sure about this, George? I might quote this argument at one of my intellectual dinner parties. I don't want to be howled down."

"No, I'm not sure."

"I think it's more likely that the tilt of the earth came first, before the need for a balanced diet. Your body, George, and mine, our bodies are probably just making the best of some mediocre cosmology. It's the same with amoebas. We're expected to believe they're incredible survivors, terrifically plucky, but in the end they've got fuck all to be pleased about, a green cell in a muddy pond. They'd be better off pulling out of the food chain totally."

"You're a bit fed up, that's all," George said after five minutes.

"It's these stamps."

"Which?"

"All of them. I need shaking up. I need a lifestyle."

"You already have one. Even I've got one."

"No I haven't."

"When was the last time you had a holiday, Gary?"

"Ten years ago."

"You could go more often."

"Or less often."

"Take my advice. Have a holiday."

"I can't, I have Deborah to look after."

Locking up was easier than opening up. He took the chains out of the safe, put the cashbox in, tugged down the shutter and snapped the locks shut. The other men in the other stalls were doing the same. They never took the trouble to say goodbye to each other, or seldom, although their Good Mornings were luxurious and regular.

Gary intended to call on Deborah when he arrived home, before Dermot returned from Brighton. He would suggest an evening in. Let me get us a take-away curry, he would say, and she would say *What a good idea,* or similar words of her choice.

In the underground he was pressed between a party of several dozen Italian schoolgirls, only two of whom were not yelling at any given moment. He tried to pass as their passive but worshiped teacher.

Gary realized something was wrong when, two minutes after re-emerging under the sky, he felt the crook of an elbow under his chin. This had never happened before. He was dragged from the range of the streetlights by the leather arm, this very tense and insistent limb.

Shortly afterwards, nothing. As they say.

Dermot was not looking forward to explaining to Geraldine how he had taken his eye off her husband for a second and lost him. On the other hand he had good news for her: Gerald was alive and had a room overlooking the sea.

In between making plans for him and Deborah (seeing her less made him think of her more) he had spent the train journey worrying that Gerald would kill himself and leave Dermot with egg on his face. If Gerald's veins were found open in his littoral refuge the coroner would have words.

Accompanying him in his carriage were a group of French schoolboys who had wispy upper lips and smart suitcases. How curiously they pronounced the names of the stations.

As he came out of the tube station an ambulance, alive with ambulance-noise, slammed past with a cargo of sick flesh.

Gwen answered Geraldine's door and brought him wordlessly to her friend by the telephone, who said, "You haven't found him, have you."

"Yes, we had a talk," he said, and sat down in an armchair. Geraldine stood up when she heard the news, whereas Gwen sat down. It looked like a game.

"Is he outside?" Geraldine asked, her voice straining with the need to know. "Where is he?"

"He seems fine. He said he felt fine."

"So he hasn't come with you."

"Not yet."

"It's a woman."

"Please calm down. It's not a woman."

She was standing in front of Dermot and their knees were almost touching. His arms were resting on the broad arms of the armchair and he was tired from the sea air.

"Does he have a telephone?"

"Why don't you take a seat."

"Yes, sit down," Gwen said.

Dermot told Geraldine what had happened and she stood through it all. When he started on his theories she sat next to his hand on the arm of the chair and let her thin straight shoulders slump into a V.

"It's good to give him a day or two to think. If you drag him back by the hair he'll go again. He was in the best possible mood, not so happy he'll never come back, happy enough not to do anything unwise, looking after himself, doing a little painting, walking around the shops."

"Don't be too hopeful," Gwen said.

"Shut up, Gwen," she said, "just shut up." And then she said "I'm sorry."

"I think that's my telephone," Dermot said, holding his arm out for silence. He walked quickly to the door and ran upstairs. He couldn't afford to waste a phone call. The ring waited for him while he found his key.

"Am I speaking to a friend of Mr. Gary Strang?"

"Yes we are friends."

"Good evening. I'm afraid he's just been brought into the casualty department."

"What's the matter with him?"

"He's quite poorly."

"Oh God." It must be his heart. Dermot always thought Gary might have too small a heart for the size of his body. Or an accident. Some car had vegetablized this innocent man.

"We always have to inform someone," she said primly.

"What's happened?"

"He seems to have been involved in a fight, but that's not for me to say."

Oh is that all. "Is he hanging around waiting to be treated?" Dermot knew what it was like in those places. Staff were short. You could knit yourself a stretcher in the time it took to be served. There was always a muddied young man in rugby knit nursing a suspect arm.

"No he's being looked after. That's not a very helpful comment. Please bring some toilet articles, a dressing gown and pajamas."

"Why, do you want me to stay with him overnight?"

"These are for him."

"I understand."

How appalling. What terrible bad luck.

Dermot remembered how he felt when Mike had finished with him (of course, it must be Mike, how *appalling*) and he multiplied the memory of that feeling to arrive at Gary's pain. Dermot was getting used to his chipped tooth, which nobody seemed to notice, and wondered what Gary would have to get used to. He considered ringing Gary's parents but decided to wait until he could give a fuller report and possibly a little background history of the hospital, if he could remember to pick up a brochure.

Gary's new bed stood against the wall and would remain there. There were pajamas in a drawer and the monogrammed dressing gown was on the door. He hesitated over the toilet requisites before emptying half the bathroom into a large plastic bag and swinging it over his shoulder. On the way out he took two oranges out of the fridge and added them to his overnight bag mainly because of their cheerful color.

"Geraldine, I have to visit Gary in hospital."

"Okay, love."

"Aren't you going to ask me why he's there?"

"Is it something unexpected?" she said distractedly.

"Oh never mind."

He left sharply. Geraldine had retreated to a small world and would not be out today. Some people could only cope with one thing at a time, fair enough. Dermot remembered what a bitch he had been when his first girlfriend went off with another boy. What a nasty business that had been.

The hospital was a long walk away through dark streets. He had never been there before but he knew the streets from great wanderings during periods of unemployment and more especially from his road-sweeping days. Dermot's favorite memory from that job was a short induction seminar on dog refuse. There were specialized techniques. You didn't rush untutored into dog refuse.

It was not a modern hospital with doors that opened automatically to preserve the energies of the sick, nor was it a converted Victorian asylum with the scratch marks of desperate fingernails etched deep under twenty coats of pain. What impressed Dermot most, as he entered the casualty department, were the signs. They were a rash on every wall. At the suggestion of a junction a dozen green or blue signposts put your mind at rest, pushing you in one direction.

The atmosphere intimidated Dermot. He didn't like to

stop one of the passing nurses in case it cost a life. They had a way of averting their eyes and moved in an aura of dynamic healing. Eventually a nurse came by at a slower speed than the rest and stood behind a desk with a sign saying Admissions, which suggested to Dermot either museums or confession.

"I think somebody's been brought in called Gary Strang. I have his personal items here."

"He's being x-rayed at the moment," she said.

"Have you seen him?"

"No I've only just come on."

"Have you spoken to anyone who's seen him?"

"Yes. I don't think he's too bad."

"I expect you see some pretty horrible injuries."

"Sometimes."

"We are all so fragile," he found himself saying.

"Excuse me," she said, heading somewhere. "Take a seat." She had been summoned by a doctor, Dermot saw, following her eyes. Nurses were vulnerable on all sides—patients hounded them, doctors did the same. And there were the relatives and friends who were constantly questioning and making audible criticisms to hide their nervousness at the illness all around.

Dermot sat and tried to see how it all fitted in. The others on the seats appeared to be as well as him. No rugby players. He hoped that at any moment a boy would be brought in with a large and ridiculous object stuck in his mouth. In due course it became clear this section was reserved for malingerers and friends, and the ambulancemen took their patients to a separate bay where they bled or lamented or just possibly died.

After half an hour Dermot was familiar with many of the nurses. He began to make a study of their knicker elastic (excluding male nurses, fat or elderly nurses. He was ashamed of this survey, particularly for its prejudices). Sometimes it went right under, which was good, but on others it dissected these women's hindquarters, making them eighths, which was bad. They glowed white, pink, blue or yellow under the uniforms.

"Excuse me," he said to one of the nurses in unimpeachable white underwear, "I've been waiting for rather a long time."

"Who for?"

"Gary Strang. All I've been told is he's rather poorly. It's too vague."

"He's having a cast put on."

"Will I be able to see him soon?"

"We'll call you when he's ready."

"So he's broken something has he?" he called, but she had already gone.

Dermot sat down again next to Gary's bag. There were many, many bones and Dermot just hoped it wasn't his thigh because Gary would look a complete farce in sawn-off trousers. It would be one of the dangly bones; as far as he knew you couldn't plaster the skull, the ribs, the shoulder blade. One question was—should Dermot be taking this seriously or was he allowed to laugh? It was never easy to pick an attitude out of the pile.

He started to read the back of Gary's shampoo. For black hair. His hair was never black.

"Are you waiting for anybody?" he asked a girl in a heavy coat.

"My friend."

"What's he in for?"

"It's a she." He was always making that mistake. Too often he thought the world was nothing but couples, roped together like mountaineers on an ice wall. "She's got trouble with her contact lenses."

"I don't know why people bother with those things."

"To see better."

"Yes, but they're just a gag nowadays. Everyone has a story about how they lost one in a lift or somewhere."

"She went to an all-night party and slept in them all day."

"An all-night party on a Monday?"

"She's in great pain." For a minute or two they watched the cream walls. "What are you doing here?"

"My friend's got unspecified injuries, he's broken something. I'm a bit worried because he takes pain badly."

Soon the woman in the heavy coat was called over and her

friend was wheeled in with two large pads of cotton wool over each eye and a crumbled mouth full of distress. Then it was Dermot's turn to be called. He was given the ward and told to follow the signs. When he arrived at the entrance to the ward he decided to wait for a nurse rather than blunder in among the wounded.

"Nurse, I've come to see Gary Strang."

"I don't think he should see anyone just yet."

"But I was sent along. I have his toothbrush and things."

"I'll take them from you," she said, doing it. "He won't be using his toothbrush this evening. He's got a broken arm, some concussion and one or two other things so it's best if you come back in the morning."

For the first time Dermot understood that something would have to be done about Mike. Ideally he should be burned in a public place, but it was more serious than that. Something really would have to be done, channels would have to be gone through.

He walked back to the casualty department and spoke to the most important-looking nurse.

"Do you ever call the police in yourself if a bad injury's brought in to you?"

"Yes. Which patient are you referring to?"

"Gary Strang."

"The police were with him when he was brought in. I'm afraid you must talk to them."

He went home and climbed to Deborah's room. She answered the door.

"You know what's happened, don't you," he said, walking in, "your boyfriend, your past, has put Gary in hospital. Don't just stand there like it's nothing to do with you."

"Oh no," she said, shutting her eyes.

"You get, you get involved with this *person* and suddenly he's in there wrecking our lives and all the time you act as if we're a pair of dumb shits from downstairs."

"Don't shout at me," she said, "just don't shout at me. What is it about you men?"

159

"Please, please," he shouted, "allow me a bit of anger, for God's sake. And don't put us in with that wild man of yours, alright, just don't pretend we're all the same, because that gets on my nerves."

"And you can stop accusing me. I moved here to get away from Mike. I changed my job so he wouldn't know where I was," (her voice was raised high by now, she was almost holding it above her head) "but someone told him, I explained it was all over, I didn't ask for your help but you decided to give it."

They stood panting at each other in the center of the room, both with red indignant eyes. Dermot thought it might be over, but she started again.

"You're sick with violence. You all behave so badly. The world is run by men and it's a disgusting place."

Dermot was sympathetic to that argument. He showed he was by saying nothing.

"How bad is Gary?" she said in the restored quietness.

"He'll probably survive. They won't let me see him until tomorrow."

"I'll come with you. I hate this as much as you, in fact I hate it more. Boys like scrapping."

"You have completely the wrong idea."

Dermot heard his telephone ringing and for the second time in an evening rushed at it before the sound died.

The police wanted to talk about Gary. They asked if he had any background information to the *incident*. He said yes and they promised to come right over.

While he waited for them he went back upstairs and invited Deborah to join him when the police arrived, and he went downstairs to warn Geraldine in case the sight of unscheduled policemen in her porch made her lose her head. Then, to relax, he went to Gary's room and tried to work out how to put his new bed together. If Gary had any concussion left over when he was released from hospital it would only be made worse by the diagrams and procedures in the instruction booklet. When you bought a piece of furniture nowadays you didn't buy a piece of furniture, you bought a stack of parts and an instruction book.

He tore at the packaging to dissipate the memory of his argument with Deborah. The assembly process was designed for two which meant it lasted twice as long as Dermot's patience. When it was done he stretched out on the cool silky diamonds of the mattress.

Geraldine showed the two policemen up nervously and Dermot kept them waiting in the hall while he went to fetch Deborah, who for some reason gave him a shy smile at the top of the stairs. He kissed her on the cheek because it seemed the right thing to do and she kissed him back on the cheek quite naturally, as if these were codes they always used.

The men didn't have their helmets with them but they were otherwise consummate policemen, tall, young and more clean-shaven than Dermot would have thought possible.

"Would you like a cup of tea?" Always tea.

"No thank you, sir. We won't stay long. Mr. Strang does live here doesn't he?" the one who talked asked Dermot and Deborah, seeing they were a couple.

"Yes," Dermot replied, leading them all into the kitchen and sitting them down. "How did it happen?"

"A lady telephoned saying there was a fracas outside her house and she was frightened to go herself and break it up. We arrived promptly but the other man had already gone, assuming it was a man."

"I think we can assume it was a man," Dermot said. "Neither of us know any women with that sort of big grudge."

"Mr. Strang said the name Mike. Do either of you know anyone by that name?"

"I used to live with him," Deborah said. "He wanted me back and Mr. Strang intervened on my behalf some days ago when he refused to leave."

"I want him locked up," Dermot said, but it sounded more like a quotation than a plea for justice. "Look at my eye." The two tall policemen leaned forward slightly. "I have a fading black eye and a chipped tooth. He did it."

Dermot wasn't happy about the way they peered so languidly. "Of course, although nothing appears to have been stolen, he may have been attacked by somebody unrelated, simply for money. What does Mr. Strang do for a living?"

"He's a stamp dealer. It's not a job that usually attracts violence."

They asked Deborah for Mike's full name, address and physical description (*Hazel eyes*, she said, as if the police were interested in eyes. Mention his huge and uncaring fists, thought Dermot) and then unfolded their long legs from under the table. They left with great courtesy.

The nurses in this hospital had Irish accents. They spoke quietly so as not to disturb Gary but he was already disturbed. He would have liked to open his eyes and put faces to voices but he felt safer this way. He knew he was lolling but he couldn't correct it.

He remembered the x-ray machine because it had cold metal arms which swung round and it seemed to be very important that he keep his own arm and head still because they wanted to take a photograph. Also he remembered smiling through clenched teeth because he understood that smiling and photography went together.

The nurses kept calling him Gary and he wondered how they knew his name. Did he look like a Gary? Dermot always said he should have been called Desmond.

He was left in a lay-by of a busy corridor while they developed the snaps, and from his trolley he heard sounds of all kinds—the laughter of nurses, wheeled vehicles making rubber screams, doors that gave soft, breathy swings, a low groaning which he discovered was his.

Gary was relieved when they wound a bandage round his arm because it showed they loved him but it was cold and sticky as if it had just been removed from a very bad wound belonging to another patient. Then his arm was not only more painful than anything he had ever felt but it was stiff as well and he panicked and cried out. At that point they began to call him Gary with real enthusiasm and regularity (Come on Gary, calm down Gary, shhh).

He must have calmed down and come on because after a while all this stopped and they wheeled him somewhere else. Sometimes, if he was lucky, someone held the doors open so his chariot could slip through noiselessly but at other times his driver banged them open with the foot of Gary's bed and they swung behind him like saloon doors.

By shutting his eyes even Gary, horizontal and not at his most perceptive, could feel the burden of evidence falling to his nose. He detected differing degrees of antisepsis in the successive rooms and corridors. At one stage it seemed they had taken him out of the hospital and parked him in a restaurant, but this turned out to be a false impression. It was suppertime, because his Irish voice (Or was it Welsh, or *was* it Irish? He had a bad headache.) asked what was being served tonight and another woman said *Lots of things.* That was the least clinical ambience but there were other places which were steeped in prophylactic smells and especially the cool room where they turned him on his front and made him count to ten.

He woke up with a stiff back and a bound hand but it wasn't the normal kind of waking up; instead he lay straddled between consciousness and unconsciousness, edging first nearer one and then nearer the other. There was a final wheeling and a number of arms lifted him onto a heavy, low bed.

His new bed. They had brought it to the hospital. How thoughtful.

Nervous was what Dermot was when the policemen had gone. Deborah was standing in the hall with her usual expression, giving him no clue what to do.

"They've gone," he said.

"So they have." He knew when she was stuck for something to say. Her voice became clipped and challenging.

"I must telephone his parents. Do you want to wait?"

"What for?"

"Let's have a quiet evening in together."

"I'm hungry."

"So am I."

"I'll get something to eat." She stepped lightly out of the hall and Dermot looked in Gary's room for his address book but he was thinking all the time of Deborah returning with steaming food which they would eat together for all the world as if they were a pair of lovers, hungry after sharing a customary evening bath and malarkey on spread towels. He kept getting images of habitualness and lazy intimacy whereas with other women they would be images of explosive and unlikely sex. It was his age, but not just his age.

Dermot hadn't met Gary's parents but had spoken to them on the telephone. Gary always described them in vignettes and as examples of various forms of human waywardness. His father was a vague man who had made his money, if Dermot was to believe Gary, by persuading elderly widows to sell him their houses cheap when they died in return for a roll of notes now. It sounded wicked but Dermot wasn't so sure—he would have taken the money and gone crazy, bought a gleaming Zimmer frame and whatever he fancied.

He found the number and dialed.

"Hello is that Mr. Strang?"

"Mr. Strang, yes it is. Who's this?"

"Dermot Povey. I live with your son."

"Dermot!"

"That's right. Dermot. I'm afraid Gary's had a bit of an accident."

"Car?" He sounded as if he had just woken up and was having to make difficult stabs at reality. In the background Dermot heard him shout lankly "Daphne, it seems Gary's been in a car accident."

"No, no, not a car," Dermot cut in.

"Not a car, you say?" In the background Mr. Strang was shouting, "No, not a car accident, apparently."

"He was sort of beaten up and he's got a broken arm and concussion."

"Poor old thing."

"Yes, it's a shame."

"Poor old thing."

"Anyway I wondered if you wanted to know the name of the hospital he's in."

He didn't seem sure at first. The telephone line fizzed, or it could have been nerve fibers connecting, fusing, connecting behind Gary's father's telephone ear. "Why?"

"To visit him."

"Will *you* be visiting him?" he asked, still dubious.

"Yes, I'm going tomorrow morning."

"In that case," he said, "maybe we should go too."

"It's up to you."

"Broken arm, you say?"

"And concussion and one or two other things."

"One or two other things," he repeated.

Dermot shortened the conversation by giving the address of the hospital and saying he looked forward to meeting Daphne and himself.

"And so do I," he said.

There were few names in Gary's address book. He was very selective about who he entered and kept a separate notebook for those addresses and telephone numbers he considered transitory. Dorothy figured in the full address book, which had Gary's name monogrammed on it just like his dressing gown. Gary still sewed small nametags onto his jumpers, scarves and jackets because he always had done. He did it so earnestly and painstakingly at the kitchen table (tearing off the cotton with his teeth with great love) that Dermot didn't mock him for it.

"Dorothy, is that you?"

"No, it's her mother. I'll just get her for you."

Dorothy must have been sitting in the same room because she was there in his ear in a second. "Dorothy speaking."

"Dermot here, Gary's friend." They used to get on well when Dorothy spent the night with Gary. When she was there Gary got it into his head to pretend he didn't care about anything. He felt he ought to be nonchalant, obviously, and one morning when eating toast he rested his feet on the cooker to emphasize this feeling. "It's about Gary. He's in hospital and I thought you might like to go and cheer him up."

"Oh *certainly*," she said wholeheartedly. "What's he having done?"

As he explained for the fourth time what had happened, Dermot hoped that the powers wouldn't release Gary from hospital before all his guests arrived with their flowers and fruit.

"Gary told me, eventually, that you had a new boyfriend," he added. "Is that still on? Still going well?"

"No," she said bluntly.

"Gary was very upset when you split up." Dermot felt bad about this phone call because Gary might get the wrong idea. He might think Dermot was calling her out of kindness, when in fact Dorothy was to take his mind off finally losing Deborah. Look at the effect it had on Mike. Made him mad.

"I was upset too."

"Seeing you there at his bedside can only help his recovery," he said piously. "I'm a little worried about the concussion."

"We must both nurse him back to health."

The door banged downstairs and Deborah brought the smell of Chinese food up and into the hall. He smiled at her (she didn't smile back) as she carried it into the kitchen in the brown carrier bag, which she supported underneath with her hand.

"Who was that?" she asked as he put the receiver down.

"Gary's girlfriend Dorothy. She insists she wants to nurse him back to health."

14th

Gary couldn't begin to describe how he felt.

He woke up during the night and again he heard groaning. It went on for some time and one barely-formed thought he had was that he should get up and ask a nurse to stop the noise so they could all get some sleep. It turned out to be him again and all he felt was that it was a good job he *hadn't* told a nurse about the groaning because he would have felt *that* small. There were dim lights all over the ward and the beds all seemed to contain bodies but there were technical difficulties associated with focusing (he couldn't do it) so he fell asleep, for something easy to do.

Although he couldn't describe how he felt there was great pressure on him to come up with a description. The nurses all wanted to know when they woke him up in spite of it being dark outside. He didn't want to say a word, ideally, until he could do justice to this thing, this giant crapulence which stretched from his bad ankle to his superbad head, the seat of his suffering, most definitely. He realized that he would probably need adjectives and clauses to shore up his story, complicated equipment, so he made do instead with a blurred request.

"Can I have pills?"

"You're already on painkillers, Gary," she said, tucking him in so tightly that the top sheet bound his chest and arms like a hawser. "How is your head?"

He just shut his eyes and shook his head. He decided not to shake his head again.

What was he doing here? How did this come to pass? His most recent memory was visiting Brighton so there was a chance that that was where it all happened, whatever it was. He may have fallen out of a train.

A woman brought him a cup of tea and put in on the table that swung out over the bed. These tables were a boon in hospitals.

Waking up after falling out of a train was like seeing the wreckage of a motorway pileup when the fog has finally cleared. Gary looked and felt for his carnage. The crux of the soreness in his bandaged right hand was at the joint of his thumb, while his forearm, which was surely broken (He had always wanted a plaster cast and to have people sign their names!), contained a shivery, radiating pain which he kept under the blanket. He would need more time to work out exactly what was going on down the left side of his back but he guessed there were ferrets under the skin there, working away. His ankle was sprained and there was his head. He was pleased that he had not damaged his face. Imagine if he had sprained his face.

"I'm sorry I couldn't think about Gary last night," Geraldine was saying, "but I had this picture of Gerald staring out to sea, all on his own."

"I understand completely. I expect Gary's already up and about and larking with the nurses."

"I'm going to wait two days and if he's not back I'll go with Gwen to talk with him, now that we know where he roughly is."

"I shouldn't take Gwen," Dermot said, when she had gone.

The conversation took place by the dustbins in the front garden. Dermot had brought the rubbish bag down, including the silver foil trays from last night, which still dripped with translucent sauce. He and Deborah had talked happily and for the first time it was he who did most of the listening. She admitted that she was lonely and did not snort derisively when Dermot said he loved her. Several times (no, all the time) he wanted to suggest they go to his room and lie down. He didn't even mind if they kept their clothes on and to him this was a measure of his seriousness. It sounded ridiculous—so he didn't say it out loud or even dare to think it with any degree of explicitness—but it would have been enough to wake up together in the morning with her breath on his ear. A funny old idea, and no two ways.

Deborah preferred him to be passive, it seemed to him. He couldn't do much more than sit around waiting for her to decide if he was worthwhile. Women had been through this for centuries, she would possibly say, if he complained about this feeling he had.

He should use Mike, be his opposite. It would be a question of showing consideration at all times, of acquiescence over small and large issues. Above all he should remain relaxed, because Mike was a coiled spring, a cocked gun.

All very well, but one of the few facts he had about Deborah's idea of charm and sexual attraction was that at one point she had moved in with Mike. She must have liked his attitude enough to put up with the parts of his character that were sick and violent. Perhaps he would do better trying to mimic Mike's brutal glamor.

All very well, but it was not so simple. He and Gary had seen Mike in circumstances that were not easy for him. Some people feel humiliated when their lovers leave them suddenly while they are away for the weekend, are shamed by their compunction to have this same lover back at all costs and, to say the least, *uneasy* when others interfere with this process, watching them plead. In the tranquillity of his home Mike may have sat in an upright chair and read sensitive poetry. It was possible that he was a scout leader one evening a week and collected for the blind at weekends. Dermot didn't want to mimic the wrong person.

The evening, in any case, had ended with a quiet goodbye and Dermot took a long time to fall asleep.

He put his rubbish away and went upstairs to ring the department store, telling them he would be in after lunch. Gary's address book was still there and he dialed George. He had met George whenever he visited Gary at work to borrow money, and the two men had been chatting away like neighbors over the garden fence. George's stand was like a stall at a jumble sale just before it closed. Gary's, on the other hand, was organized and plump with produce.

George took the news very badly. The two of them were very close (three or four yards in business hours). How could someone do such a thing, George said.

Dermot recradled the receiver and became shaky, the sign that he was about to meet Deborah.

They walked to the hospital and both said how nervous they were at what they would find. She had makeup on and smart stiff shoes which tapped on the pavement like coconut halves. He was growing aware of the subtleties of her face, of the hatching on her lips and a small pale mole under one eyebrow. Fortunately, she seemed not to mind him looking at her face as if it were the small print of a contract and she continued to keep strict time with her heels.

"Please don't ask him many questions," a nurse said. "He's had a bang on the head."

"That can't do it any good, can it," Dermot said, to show he understood perfectly.

They went into Gary's section of the ward and scanned the four beds in respectful silence, as if they were looking for a shrine in a church. The hospital was like a church. It had hush and a larger than average number of people at the thin ends of their lives. There was a chaplain on call and wise old prophets called consultants.

All four beds were asleep and Gary looked the most asleep, with his eyes screwed shut and his body up to its nose under sheets. The other three were dozing, their arms draped at odd angles on the blanket.

"Do you think we should wake him?" Deborah whispered. The three men woke instantly, their eyes snapping open. One had an aperture at the base of his throat, a tracheotomy like a bullet hole. Dermot had an uncle with one and this uncle would open his shirt at Christmas and show all his young nephews, just as some uncles do tricks with matches. Dermot's mother allowed him to do this to scare her boys off tobacco but she always sent her daughters out of the room and now they smoked like chimneys.

The other men had invisible disorders and many get-well cards. The articles arranged on their bedside tables looked like fixtures: Dermot feared these mute men would never leave. There was a family photograph in a silver frame and he had to look away.

"I'm sure they would have told us if we weren't to wake him," he said, but they sat down by his bed and did nothing. The three other men drifted back into sleep.

"It's a nice clean ward," Deborah breathed into his ear.

"I hate these places."

Gary then broke the surface of his white sheets and laid his plastered arm in the open, murmuring a tired "You're here," as if to imply they should have gone hours ago.

"You're looking well Gary," Dermot smiled and said.

"I feel like shit."

"And you still have your sense of humor!"

"No, I do actually feel that way."

"So what happened?" That was one question already. He must learn to talk in statements.

"I thought I fell out of a train but now I'm not so sure." Dermot wasn't alarmed. He had consulted his book of Medical Knowledge and one possible symptom of concussion was the temporary loss of the most immediate memories. The book's accuracy on this point may have been a piece of luck because it was unreliable on nosebleeds and no help on hangovers, his two major maladies.

"You told the policeman Mike was involved," he explained very clearly as if Gary was mad or very old. There was a long pause.

"It was Mike. I remember now."

"Hello Gary. I'm so sorry this has happened."

"Hello Deborah."

"That's a sweet nightdress you have on."

"It's a nightshirt," he said heavily. "It ties up at the back."

"I brought your pajamas in," Dermot insisted.

"I can't get my cast through the armhole."

"I see there's a bandage on your hand."

"They tell me the webbing is torn. I didn't know I had any webbing." He had enough energy to talk but none left over for expression, even for the parsimonious amount with which he usually spiced up his speech.

"Are they looking after you properly?" Deborah asked.

"They're angels. I love these nurses." His face clouded over and then cleared. "Sign my arm."

"How do you mean?"

"You know, sign my arm, like people do."

Dermot went to the man with the hole in his throat, to show he was not scared (he wanted in due course to tell him about his uncle and the fun they had at Christmas, in order to cheer him up) and asked if he could borrow the pen next to his jug of water. He nodded. The ward was awake again now and people were moving about the corridors wheeling their drips ahead of them like supermarket trolleys, coughing and talking.

"What shall we put?"

"Anything."

He gave the pen to Deborah and she inscribed on the hard white curve MY BRAVE SOLDIER BEST WISHES DEBORAH X X. Dermot took a long time to think and finally came up with GET WELL SOON DERMOT POVEY.

"I can never think of anything," he said.

Gary knew he had a reputation for being a difficult patient. Dermot wouldn't let him forget the time he threw a bowl of cornflakes across the kitchen when he had a heavy cold, screaming that he couldn't taste a thing. This time he was going to be a stoic. At the same time he wanted everyone to know that his were not ordinary agonies. All those who waved away the anesthetist and submitted cheerfully to amputation and ectomy and serious disorders—they were not braver than him, they simply *had higher pain thresholds*. He had a very low one, it was right there among the lowest. How much more impressive, therefore, that he should be making so little fuss.

"Nurse, you'll have to do something about my bloody back."

"It's bound to be sore. You've had stitches."

"How many?"

"Probably more than a dozen."

"Is that more than most people or less?" he wanted to know.

"It's a fair number."

"You mean it's less."

"You must be on the mend, the way you've perked up," she said, pumping up one of the patient's pillows.

"I've only perked up to tell you how bad I feel."

She went away and the throbbing returned to his head. There was a small bump on his *occiput*. The occiput, according to his doctor, was the back of the head. They had a careless habit of giving sobriquets to most parts of the body—he had not, though it felt like it, broken his arm. What he had under the plaster was a fractured *ulna*. Until he came here he thought Ulna was a Mediterranean islet, so you gained from coming to hospital once in a while. The doctor had been young and in a hurry but Gary wouldn't let him go until he had explained exactly what had happened to his body. He wanted to make a list but Dermot had given the pen back and he couldn't write anyway because of this debilitating seediness he felt. The stitches on his back were apparently designed to knit together skin that had been opened like a knife through butter by broken glass. It looked like he had rolled on a bottle which is a dangerous thing to do and completely inadvisable. His ulna was fractured probably by him "falling awkwardly" to quote the doctor and Gary considered it self-explanatory that the fall had been awkward but he supposed it was a case of set phrasing like "died peacefully" and "myself personally." His torn webbing had been stitched at the same time as his back, while they had the cotton out, and he was told not to splay his hand for a week or two unless he wanted to see blood seeping through the bandage. They were keeping him in for a couple of days until his head stopped aching (heads had to be watched) and until he would be able to lead a normal life at home, boil an egg, pull on his socks without a leg-up from a second party.

173

There was a frisson when two policemen walked into the ward in their uniforms. Gary was not surprised to see them because this was a hospital of uniforms. They should have passed unobserved.

"Hello Gary," the one that talked said. Christian names for invalids and children and old cons. "We brought you in yesterday. Is it alright if we ask you some questions?"

"If my nurses say yes that's good enough for me." These men were a soothing presence. Since receiving these injuries Gary had been concerned that the world as a whole was dissolving into anarchy. The police were known for their tough line on anarchy, they were really not fond of it. He wanted this anarchy business sorted out before the doctors made him leave the hospital because they needed the bed.

"What do you remember about the attack?"

"It was definitely Mike. I don't know his surname. I remember his face because when he had finished he looked at me quite anxiously. I don't think he meant to go this far. He seemed to want to start again and this time, you know, do it more gently."

"We've been to see him."

"I want him punished, mind you," he said, to correct any impression.

"He can't verify his movements and his boots have left prints on the mud where we found you. We'll probably charge him with assault."

"That's wonderful news." Gary just wanted Mike out of the way. He didn't care how they did it or even whether it was Mike himself who decided he had run out of wrath. It didn't feel like wonderful news, particularly, but Gary thought it was possible he would build up a bigger head of revenge when he added up the discomfort and the financial sacrifice. There was no money in staying in hospital.

The policemen said goodbye and as they left they were dissected by Dorothy, who looked over her shoulder at them. She sat down on the bed itself rather than on one of the chairs provided for visitors. The policemen hadn't sat on the bed, nor had Dermot and Deborah, but she did it with such conviction that it suddenly became the most obvious place.

"Let me kiss you."

It was nice of her to kiss him. He felt much more at ease with Dorothy than Deborah. Ease was more important to him now. It was easier.

"I'm glad you've come," he said. "You didn't have to wear black."

"I didn't know how bad you would be. Which would you like, bananas or apples?" She rustled inside a carrier bag.

"Why can't I have both?"

"I haven't offered you both. Alright have both."

"I didn't mean it. You take me too seriously."

"Fancy you saying a thing like that."

"It's probably the concussion."

She had not changed. Gary always thought of Dorothy as very English but she had a foreign complexion which Dermot described as avocado, not that it was green or anything. To Gary very-English meant that she could never do anything to astonish him. She wouldn't want to.

"I'm not sitting on your legs, am I?"

"No, you're fine."

"You were wincing."

"It's a side effect of men in my condition. Dermot rang you, did he?"

"I was thinking of phoning you anyway."

Gary was glad she'd come, that much was true. Dermot must be pleased with the way things were working out, him turning up with Deborah looking like a bride and groom in makeup and clean shirt respectively while Dorothy is summoned away from her new and expert lover to sit at the bedside of the crabby former lover during his little bit of trouble. But let him tell Dermot something—Dorothy wasn't any port in a storm, he had been receptive to her from the evening they met. (On Saturday nights people talked to each other in underground stations. "Is this right for Baker Street?" she had shouted from the opposite platform. "No, you should be on this side with me." "I thought this was right for Baker Street." "Believe me, it's this platform you want." It was late at night and there couldn't have been more than forty people listening to this chitchat over the ghostly jangling of the rails. She could easily have asked somebody on her own platform, but when she arrived warm and breathless by his side, with a beaded forehead from the climb across the footbridge, he was pleased she had spoken to him.)

They talked until Gary's lunch was brought in. She kissed him lightly on the lips and went back to work, taking both the apples and the bananas with her, presumably by mistake.

Dermot picked his suit up from the dry cleaners, trying to stay as long as possible in the shop because he loved its chemical air. He wore it to the launderette and was the cleanest and smartest customer in there by a long way. Deborah had gone off to make sandwiches. An old gentleman offered to help him fold his sheets when they finally stopped bucking and flopping around in the tumble dryer but his rheumatoid hands made it difficult for him to hang onto the corners of the sheets, which twice slipped onto the floor. There was nothing you could do about old age, nothing at all. It swallowed you up.

The second post brought him his first mail for days, a postcard from his sister saying she could find him a job on a rig. To help him make up his mind she had chosen a card showing Aberdeen town center lashed by rain.

He went into Gary's room, found his questionable black sheets in their packets and fitted them over the new bed with a strange sense of ceremony.

When he arrived at work he explained where he had been that morning and they all clucked about violence.

As he worked through the afternoon Dermot looked out for a book for Gary. He liked cartoons and sometimes recipe books, though in these it was the photographs he liked above all else and when cooking he rarely bothered to bring together more than half the ingredients, in fact he would miss the cheese out of macaroni and cheese, the beef out of Mexican Beef Stew. Audacious. Maps were a complete irrelevance in Gary's life but he would on occasions unfurl on the kitchen table a new map he had bought and study the Great Lakes or Borneo with attention, as if he was going out on the next plane. None of these interests was especially appropriate so Dermot bought a copy of *Aikido—Self-Defence in the Modern World*.

There was a conspiracy of silence between the four men in Gary's bay which he was glad of. He had all these visitors to talk to already.

"Your mother's in the car," his father said. "You know what she's like in hospitals."

"How can anyone know. She always waits outside."

"Hah!"

They seldom met face to face but the two generations often telephoned each other, young speaking unto old, old getting it terribly wrong.

"Is that a new mustache, dad?"

"You mean this one?"

It was more tiring when he had to ask his visitors questions. He assumed his father was a different man when he was with his free-signing elderly widows. The spiv must be just below the surface.

"How's business?"

"Ticking over. I see you've done something to your arm."

"Snapped a bone."

"Some kind of a fight was it? Your friend on the telephone didn't have a full grasp of the facts."

Dermot's been through my address book, Gary was thinking. I'll have everyone I've ever known passing through this ward. It will be like drowning.

"Here, dad. Write your name and message on my arm."

"What's this, some kind of game?"

He pulled a dainty lacquered fountain pen out of his tweed jacket and leant over, pulling Gary's exposed fingers so that the arm would be at the right angle for him to sign. For a minute they stayed in this position of unaccustomed intimacy, hand in hand, Gary feeling odd while his father noticed nothing as usual, concentrating as he was on writing his deliberate message. ALL THE BEST FROM YOUR FATHER AND MOTHER IN HERTFORDSHIRE, Gary recited approvingly but expected people would think he had parents in other counties as well.

"I suppose I ought to go and see your mother in the Rover. You know what she's like about waiting in cars."

"Say hello for me."

"Most certainly. Cheerio."

He slept for about an hour and awoke to find visitors grouped around the other beds. They looked over at him and he only hoped he hadn't been groaning. He smiled, they smiled. It was not easy to decide which caucus to listen to first and in the course of this important decision he fell asleep, waking up to find them gone.

His headache had become quiet and did no more than hum to itself in the dark beneath his skull. Above his left shoulder there hung a length of plastic and a dial. Gary thought it was a medical device of some kind that they stuck into your body when the need arose, but under examination it proved to be a radio. He hooked on the earpiece and found the hospital's own station, whose presenter was performing very well for someone who had clearly just come round after an operation. He played records and stumbled through requests for Ivys and Alberts and Harriets who were all ill but would be getting better. The Friends of the Hospital were holding a bazaar and Gary made up his mind there and then to contribute to that bazaar; he would drop back with a bottle of whiskey next week and the nurses would gather around him, flirting and saying how clean-cut he looked with clothes on.

Here was George with flowers.

"What a terrible experience for you." He looked consumed with worry. Gary realized that his other guests hadn't seemed very concerned. They may have thought this out in advance and began to look concerned only when they left the ward, thinking *What a state HE was in.*

"Never mind. We all get beaten up in the end."

"I hope not."

"How was work today?"

"It's unusual not having you to talk to. I kept asking questions and not getting answers. I've brought you a stamp magazine to read."

"Don't look so worried, George."

"Do I look worried?"

"You were saying yesterday I needed a holiday. The chambermaids here are very attentive and we have a television lounge."

"But it's not exactly the same."

"It's not *exactly* the same."

Gary asked the nurse who came in with his cloudy medication if he could have a vase. She told him he should use the sterilized plastic beaker like everybody else and George looked offended by her small joke, as if she really was a chambermaid who had gone a little too far. She came back with an institutional-looking vase, this was after all an institution, and George arranged the flowers with a great deal more flair than he used when selling stamps. Now they all had flowers.

"This rather sets our dinner party back," George said, still extremely worried.

"It does. You should have seen me struggling over lunch. I had to call a nurse over to dice it for me."

"They shouldn't be giving you tough meat in your state."

"No, this was bread and butter pudding. My arms are still quivery and I've got some torn webbing," he said proudly.

George sat back on his chair and looked around. "I see the nurses dress in all different colors. They wore uniforms in the last hospital I visited."

"They are uniforms George, be your age." The strength was coming back into his voice. Soon he would be able to bellow and roar again. "Each color means something different, they tell me. Pink is for beginner nurses before they get their license or whatever, and then they're allowed to wear pale blue and then white when they really know what they're doing. I may have got the shades mixed up."

"Some of them are wearing orange."

"That's the catering department. The orange people aren't allowed to touch the patients, they can't take temperatures or draw on the charts at the ends of the beds."

Even after these few hours Gary knew certain routines. He loved having his pulse taken. The feel of cool fingers on his wrist. Nurse counting off the seconds on her pocket watch. He wasn't so happy about having the thermometer in his mouth because he had a permanent desire to crunch the glass, even though he just *knew* he wouldn't like the taste of mercury. In spite of this quirk he enjoyed hospital life and wished he had a lingering virus and not these injuries, which started off as raw torture but would improve predictably. The hospital had a shop on the ground floor and a bank and needless to say a well-stocked chemist, so you could say it was a microcosm of the big world.

"What's that you're wearing, Gary, some kind of blouse?"

"It's a hospital nightshirt, please don't call it a blouse."

"I have a spare pair of pajamas if you need any."

"I can't get my own jacket over my cast," he explained again. "We had another go just after lunch. The nurse pulled the curtain round and we tried to squeeze the jacket over together but no luck."

"Are you sure about the pajamas? Mine may have baggier arms."

"Even if your jacket is baggier you're about six inches shorter than me, George. I don't want to look like the victim of a hit-and-run tailor. I've given Dermot some money and he's going to look for pajamas with wide arms in his shop."

Gary saw Geraldine and Gwen looking through the glazed partition as he spoke. Gwen was still wearing a transparent rain hat which was tied tightly under her chin. She often sported this accessory just to be on the safe side even before it began to rain. It was a theory of Dermot's that if she had her rain scarf on rain was impossible.

"George, meet my landlady Geraldine and our neighbor Gwen."

Gwen doffed her hat and spent a minute or two folding it into small squares and putting it into her handbag. They all watched her doing this, as if it were an origami master class.

"We have George to thank for these lovely flowers," he said in the limp but formal language of gratitude.

"I work with Gary," he explained, as Gwen nudged Geraldine to open up her own bag. "He's marvelous to work with."

"Oh tush. You wouldn't like me to blush in front of the girls."

"We also have flowers," Geraldine said. Now she reminded him of a trade delegation unpacking gifts.

"Nobody's ever brought me flowers before," he said, sniffing them through the paper.

"Yes, I did," George said in a small voice.

Gary sent Gwen off in search of another vase and she came back with what was most certainly a specimen jar. Either the hospital was undervased or this was the proof he needed of Gwen's ability to attract ridicule with no effort. This was not cruelty, Gary thought—though people were cruel—it was an attempt to tear at her veils of despondency and complaint.

"Did Dermot tell you about Gerald?" Geraldine had been waiting to ask from the beginning.

"He said he found him. It's a strange affair."

"I'm sure it's nothing I've done," she explained to them all. George's face was politely perplexed. "It's my husband," she said to him. "He's gone to Brighton for a few days to get away from it all."

"You realize of course," Gary said, "that it was the man we met on Sunday who attacked me."

"How wicked," Gwen said.

"He did look jittery," said Geraldine. "Do you think I should have a word with Deborah about him?"

"It's not her fault."

"Maybe I should ask her to leave."

"Find alternative accommodation," Gwen said.

"No, don't do that." He wanted Deborah to stay, hoping she would want to nurse him back to health. It *was* her fault, when you looked at it. If Dorothy, let's say, had pulled Deborah off the pavement and bashed her about Gary would not have hesitated to help her while she recovered. With no medical knowledge whatsoever he would gladly have taken on the burden of dressing and undressing her and bathing her bruises while making sure her plaster of Paris did not melt in the water. What could this injury do but bring them closer to each other? What did war wives do when their men were away fighting, harvesting wounds in foreign fields? Some of them, of course, slept with the men who stayed at home.

Dermot realized on his way home that he had forgotten to look for wide-armed pajamas in the menswear department. This was a dereliction of duty. *Forgotten to* was not quite right—he had put the thought out of his mind as knowingly as he would have put the cat out before going to bed. He had spent the generous money that was marked down for pajamas with wide arms on two steaks, salad, grapes, a bottle of wine, a carton of orange juice and a new shirt, which he had bought in the menswear department just along from the pajama counter. That was how derelict his duty was.

As he arrived home with his packages Geraldine and Gwen were about to leave for the hospital. Geraldine was worried about leaving the telephone on its own and Gwen was putting on her gloves in front of the hall mirror. Dermot noticed how different she looked in reflection. People do not see themselves the way they are.

"We're just off," Geraldine said to Dermot.

"Have you got the flowers?" Gwen asked into the mirror with her new, alien mouth.

Dermot went upstairs, slipped into his shirt and gave the food to the fridge. To pass the time until Deborah arrived he poured himself a glass of wine and played patience with Gary's cards. He couldn't remember the rules and sat for some time simply listening to the refrigerator going on and off with the cards frozen in his hands. He fetched Gary's book on *Aikido—SDITMW* and read about the acquisition of total physical control. The emphasis was on subduing the attacker without injuring him and there were photographs of large men looking as subdued as subdued, pinioned by svelte women. Dermot flattened the book by wedging it in a half-open drawer and imitated some of the positions and the expressionless faces of the self-defendants.

"Hai!" he shouted. "Euh!"

He sat down again and before long there was a knock from Deborah. She moved brightly and had taken off the makeup she had been wearing in the hospital.

"What have you got for me?" she asked and Dermot threw open the fridge with a laugh, laying the food out on the table in front of her. "I look at food all day," she said, looking at it.

She nevertheless helped prepare the meal while Dermot cooked the steak over a demonic flame that licked his hand and sent sparks into the air. Deborah looked across anxiously, watching his mad agitations of the pan. He got this way when he cooked.

She didn't ask him where things were kept but instead opened the high cupboard doors, standing on one foot, and looked for herself. From the neatness inside she withdrew what interested her.

She didn't ask him how he liked his salad and he failed to consult her on how she liked her steak. The serving was delayed because Dermot went to look for a candle, which he eventually found, and a candlestick, which he did not. The candle was laid at an angle inside a beer mug and dripped wax on the table.

Her sharp white teeth made light of the meat, which was crisp on the outside but red within, so red he thought it was a drop of blood he saw escape from the corner of Deborah's mouth before meeting the back of her hand.

Dermot only emptied half the bottle of wine during the meal because of Deborah's views on alcoholism. He wanted to drink it all but feared the first slur.

The candle had to be transferred from the beer mug into a sherry glass and they started to pluck at the bowl of grapes with slow movements of their hands.

"What is it that makes you want to sleep with me?" she asked.

"Does it make you feel used, having people wanting to sleep with you?"

"It makes me feel like everything else I do and say is a waste of time."

"It's not the *only* thing men want. It's the *first* thing, that's all. The difference is that I want to be with you all the time. I'd want to work with you, come home on the same bus, stay at home with you until the next morning and then go to work with you again the following morning. I'm sorry if that's not what you want to hear."

"I don't like obsessive behavior."

"I'm being completely rational. You're being obsessive."

"How?"

"You're obsessed about not giving yourself away."

"Not really."

"I have no idea what you're thinking about."

"You don't ask direct questions."

"Do you love me?"

"I didn't say I was always going to answer them."

He was glad she hadn't answered. If she had said yes he would not have believed her. If she had said no he would not have accepted it.

"Tell me about Mike."

She narrowed her eyes and thought hard, as though it had all happened a long, long time ago.

"He had a very deliberate way of doing things. I think that's why I've learnt to be careful what I say now. I would make casual remarks and he incorporated them into our relationship. He clubbed me to death with them."

"For example?"

"I once told him that I thought Sunday night was the best night to go to the cinema, so he insisted that we always go on Sunday nights from then on. Just after he met me I told him that I loved him."

"Couldn't you change your mind?"

"No. He thought that if you said a thing it was scratched in stone. He latched onto words that he liked the sound of. He liked the sound of me saying *I love you.*"

"It does have a certain ring to it."

"I only thought it for a split second. You can't go on that. Mike has a mind like, I don't know, like a large-print library book—I liked the clear way he said things but once I'd read him there wasn't much more I could say."

"So why did you take up with him?"

"I thought he was strong and silent. He turned out not to be silent enough. I wanted someone to look after me."

"Why?"

"Haven't you noticed how women like to be looked after?"

"In this day and age?"

"I don't mean they want to be treated like housewives. But they want someone standing beside them who's strong."

"And silent."

"Not in all cases."

"What is it that makes you want to sleep with me?" Dermot asked. His blood stopped in his veins, hung in the ventricles of his heart.

She did not lift an eyebrow.

"Because you seem alright. You've been so earnest."

The blood moved again, slithering exultantly down its red corridors.

"How long have you wanted to?"

"I don't know. I've had a lot on my mind. Gerald and so on. I've got a job going nowhere and an old boyfriend who won't let go. I'm twenty-five. And you've been shadowing me at a time when I've found the thought of sex less interesting than at any other time in my life."

"I'm sure it's only a temporary phase."

"It is. It's over. I want to sleep with you."

"You're not just saying you want to on the spur of the moment?"

"I think the mood will last me a while. Men leave women more often than women leave men."

"Is that true?"

"I don't know. It shouldn't be."

He picked up her hands from the table and for the first

time he felt her responding to the pressure of his fingers. She clasped him with her own cool fingers.

"Deborah, what will happen to us afterwards?"

"I'll probably go to the bathroom and you'll fall asleep."

"No, I mean after that."

"You'll wake up and want to do it again more slowly, trying out other tricks."

"You're not being serious."

"I've *been* serious."

"You told me you only got involved with men who had enough money to entertain you."

"You know very well I was lying." She released one of her hands and plucked a grape.

It was only eight o'clock but they went to Gary's bedroom, because of his fresh clean sheets and the tempting virginity of the bed, and when the curtains had been drawn they stood close to each other and took off their clothes. Dermot once reached out to touch her but it interrupted the rhythm they each had and had always had for removing their clothes. He withdrew his fingers from her creamy breasts and his thumbs from her brown nipples. She lay on top of the sheets and watched him as he had watched her face on the way to the hospital, except it wasn't his face she was studying.

Dermot could not get over this. They were moving together, clawing, moaning.

Later they woke up and did it again more slowly, trying out other tricks.

15th

"You know yesterday evening?" Dermot asked, lying on one elbow in bed.

"What?" Deborah replied. She was lying face down and Dermot had slid the sheets up over her legs so that they were gathered around her back. Anyone else would have looked ridiculous.

"You said *I've had a lot on my mind. Gerald and so on.* What did you mean?"

She seemed to think about keeping the truth to herself but it was pointless lying to someone who had their hands resting between your legs.

"I know about Gerald."

"What about him?"

"Everything. He used to draw me."

Gary plugged the earpiece in as the sun came up through the window, hitting Mr. Grimes opposite. Mr. Grimes was dribbling slightly but it did not distress Gary unduly because he himself sometimes woke up with a well of saliva lying beside him on the pillow, and so did Dorothy. The orifices ooze whether we like it or not, he believed that was half of their charm and purpose.

"Hallo, this is, um, Hospital Radio. Coming to you from ... the basement of the ... hospital. Hallo. Hospital Radio. Er."

"He'll never make Radio Four," Gary shouted to the waxen-face Mr. Turville, diagonally opposite. "Not in a million years will he make Radio Four."

187

Mr. Turville didn't know what he was talking about and thought he was possibly having a *turn*.

Gary started to sing along to "My Boy Lollipop."

Neither Gary nor Dermot had asked Deborah how she had found out that Gerald and Geraldine had a room to let. Dermot guessed that they had advertised in a newsagent's window (among cards selling unwanted pets and items of sad-sounding furniture, next to a printed invitation to contact Samantha, who claimed she was a baby doll). But no. The first time Gerald had seen Deborah she was completely naked. It is one of the very few occasions when you meet someone for the first time in this way. There were nine of them in the class and they drew her in their different ways, some of them with feathery movements of the charcoal, others like Gerald in a few very determined lines. She had the gift of stillness. At one point she asked if she could be allowed to close her eyes and after some discussion they allowed her to, but it seemed that it was too difficult even for someone as immobile as Deborah to stand up perfectly still with her eyes closed, so she opened them again.

Gerald was one of only two men and he took his classes too seriously at first to be distracted by anything other than the pursuit of excellence in drawing. Admittedly, he had expected the life model to be a little more middle-aged, a little more like his wife or like real people, with flesh sagging and bulging more than perhaps it should in one or two places. They had had other models, including a man with a large penis, which six of the women in the group had all scaled down for decency's sake while one woman had scaled it up for reasons of her own.

After the first session with Deborah had finished she disappeared behind a screen, dressed and said goodbye with a cheerful wave as the rest of the class gathered up their papers. Gerald was stirred by her presence. He considered that the purpose of art was to create beauty and he should not be ashamed at feeling that it was more likely to be created by painting her rather than two peaches and a banana. In his thorough studies of art books from the gallery's shop, which he was allowed to borrow and read in his lunch break as a result of a kindness by the staff there, he had found corroboration in other famous artists, who chose particular models because they inspired them.

Gerald didn't expect to see her again but she came for another session a week later and as he shaped her on the crisp paper he started to see her as an icon which he wanted to be able to draw at will. He was a reticent man and would not have thought of approaching her, so he was more than pleased when she stayed afterwards to look at the way she had come out on the nine large white pages and to chat with the group. She asked if anyone knew of a place she could move into and Gerald said he had a bedsit in his house. Fearing that it all sounded hopelessly dubious, he added *I'm sure my wife would be delighted to have you.*

"Does he have any talent?" Dermot asked when she had finished explaining. They were eating again, this time in bed. Dermot dropped a piece of toast on the sheets, where it joined the other fresh stains. They started laughing at the mess they were creating.

"I don't know, but I like his pictures of me. The trouble is that he's adopted me as a sort of idol. I feel terrible pressure." Her face darkened. "I shouldn't have moved in but I was desperate to get away from Mike. I've had to deceive Gerald's wife, you know. She thinks we met at the gallery."

"So you know where Gerald is, then." Dermot lay with his head on Deborah's stomach and stroked his hand under the crook of one of her knees. He heard the whoosh and burble of her tubes. He had heard the sound of her entrails and been inside her and now he only had her mind to open up very slightly.

"He's written to me several times at work, asking if I think he'll ever be recognized as a painter."

"They'll recognize him as one if he keeps getting paint in his hair."

"He swore me to secrecy. I was worried about him so much one evening that I went down to see him."

"That was when you said you had spent the night with a friend."

"He is a friend."

"I hope he slept in the bath."

"He put me up in a hotel."

"He'll have to come back, you know."

"I know."

Mr. Pantelides was finding it hard to stay awake as Gary talked at him from the neighboring bed.

"Take the 1929 £1 Postal Union Congress stamp. I sold one last year for £750 in perfect condition."

"That's a lot of money," Mr. Pantelides managed to remember to say, barely audibly.

"A lot? Did you say a lot of money?"

Mr. Pantelides realized he had made a mistake.

"You're joking, aren't you," he said, brandishing with his good arm the stamp magazine that George had brought him. "I was selling it for the same price three years ago. I mean you have to be joking, seriously."

His companion nodded off and Gary remained in his bed and waited as the others slept around him. Two hours later Mr. Grimes woke up and before he registered he was awake Gary was asking him how many stitches he had had.

"I've had more than a dozen," Gary explained.

Dermot and Deborah knocked on the door and Gerald showed no surprise when he found their two heads silhouetted against the darkness of the English Channel. They followed him up two flights of stairs to his room, which was as Dermot had expected it to be—thick with the smell of paint and strewn with paper and canvases, on his bed and table, propped up against walls, everywhere. There was little evidence that somebody actually lived there. A cold cup of coffee and the uneaten crust of a piece of toast. Dermot hated it when people didn't eat their crusts.

"I'm sorry about this," Deborah said to Gerald.

"You don't need to be."

"Nice to see you, Gerald," Dermot said.

The three of them wandered awkwardly around the room

for a while. Dermot and Deborah looked at the pictures and drawings while Gerald trailed after them.

"I don't suppose you have a cup of coffee, do you?" Dermot asked.

"We'll have to share a cup."

"I don't mind. Deborah?"

"No, I don't mind."

"We're happy to share a cup, Gerald."

Dermot had no idea about art. Like most people, in the welter of civilization he had lost the instinctive ability to know, cleanly and clearly, what he liked. The skill was lost forever on the first day of civilization, when two cave men started talking together in front of the same hunting scene on a cave wall. In any case what Gerald needed at this moment was not a critical analysis of his work. He didn't know what Gerald needed. Dermot accepted the way the world was and ideally if a man decided he wanted to run away then that was what was best for him. Where did his responsibilities to himself start to shade into the commitment he owed to his wife? Wasn't it just that Gerald had *handled matters badly,* in other words it was a question of technique?

"Why are you doing this, Gerald," Dermot asked.

A pause began to grow, soon filling the room like a large plant.

Gerald sat down. "I don't know," he began to say. "I don't know, I don't know. It's nothing. I don't know."

Dermot hoped that if he waited long enough the truth would flop out of Gerald's mouth and lie there on the floor for them all to look gawp at.

He opened his mouth. "It's all, it's all about making something," he said very slowly. "I wanted to make something before they, you know, before I ... It's become quite ... an important ... thing." He stood up and started walking around, translating his agitation into little steps this way and that on the strewn carpet. He held his palms out in a gesture of confusion, his wrists against his chest and his eyes wide. "I don't know what the point of everything is otherwise. At the gallery I

191

stand with paintings which have...power. And then I come home to Geraldine and she makes the world...small, silly."

(And Dermot thought *It is silly. What are you saying?*)

Deborah said, "You should come home and share the experience with your wife. Don't you think *she* has the same feelings sometimes."

"No I don't."

"How do you know?"

"I used to paint a little and I showed her a picture once."

"Didn't she like it?"

"It wasn't that she didn't like it. She just didn't understand at all. She stood there laughing."

Dermot knew what he meant. Enthusiasms are made of a delicate fiber. In his time he had recommended books that he loved and they had been read and handed back to him with disdain and incomprehension, as if they were dead fish.

"She didn't know you felt so strongly."

"That's part of it. She has no sensitivity."

"But what about you, Gerald?" Dermot said. "You never talk to her. When she was fifty, that time, she was in a terrible state about it. About growing old and you not helping her."

He said nothing and did not make the coffee.

"If you get married in this day and age and it doesn't work," he eventually said, "you just break up and start again. Do you know what it's like to choose the wrong person and to be married to her for thirty years?"

He did not want to go on, sat down, got up abruptly and then sat down again.

"It was meeting Deborah that made me have to take some kind of stand. I didn't have any...hopes...for her." He trailed off.

There are some people, Dermot thought as he saw Deborah's profile on the edge of his vision, who, often without meaning to, bring others to crisis.

Gerald had never talked so much. You could have collected up all the words he had spoken over the whole previous ten years and put them in a book and they would barely have added up to a preface.

"What kind of stand?" Dermot asked.

"I don't know. I thought that if I could capture her properly I would be happy. If I can't then I might give up."

Capture was right. That was exactly what you had to do.

"What are your chances?" Dermot asked.

Gerald walked slowly to a door Dermot had not noticed and opened it. In the room behind it there were probably thirty drawings and paintings of Deborah scattered about the room and one on an easel.

"I'm doing my best," he said.

A minicab was called and the woman on the phone did not sound too surprised when Dermot asked if they could be driven to London. He supposed that there were many occasions when a dirty weekend in Brighton went so badly wrong that a taxi away was a small price to pay, though it was a large price to pay. He asked for a car with a big boot.

The lights were going out all over Brighton as they swung away. Gerald was in the front, his bullish head staring out straight ahead and his ears lit up orange by the streetlamps. They turned red when their car stopped at the traffic lights and then green again as they moved off. In the back was a plastic bag containing the essentials Gerald had had to buy and a larger bag with painting equipment. Dermot's thighs were weighed down by canvases and his mouth was dry from the coffee he had never had. On his left shoulder Deborah was resting her head, her eyes closed.

Dermot smiled.

16 th

Gary would say nothing. Only this. If Dermot had been in hospital with multiple injuries he would have visited him every day for at least the first two days, probably the third day and maybe the fourth as well, though he would not be bringing flowers or fruit by that stage. That was all he was saying.

The nurses had told him that he was well enough to go home that morning. He had hobbled to the telephone to ask Dorothy if she would come to take him home, as Dermot and Deborah had abandoned him. The warmth in her voice almost made his own voice crack.

It felt like the doctors had stapled the skin of his back together with long, rusty iron staples, rather than sewn it. He was beginning to wonder if they had left something inside his hand when they sewed *that* up. Mr. Pantelides was openly ignoring him. The papers had arrived late. Dermot had not brought his new pajamas.

He was told that someone wanted to speak to him on the telephone and he asked the nurse if she would bring it to his bed. She told him she would not and he shouted "Why not?" Mr. Grimes put his spare pillow over his head. "And you've set my arm at an angle," he added irritably after banging it by accident on Mr. Pantelides's bed as he made his way slowly to the telephone at the end of the ward.

"Gary, I'm sorry we couldn't see you yesterday," Deborah was saying.

"Don't you worry about me. We're having a whale of a

time in here, aren't we lads." He held the receiver up to the ward and the three sick men said nothing. "As you can hear. Mr. Turville is leading the dancing."

"Dermot and I were bringing Gerald back from Brighton."

"Good."

"I wanted to say that I'd like to move in with Dermot." She was calling from a public phone box and the tight cabin made her voice sound hot and small.

Gary answered quietly. "Well, there you have it."

Deborah was hesitant. "Is that alright?"

"Do you want me to move out?" Gary asked. "I'm not going to. I just wanted to know whether you wanted me to."

"No, no. Stay. I forgot to ask how you were feeling."

A bus made its way past the booth.

"Do you want to ask now?" he asked.

"Don't be hard on me, Gary. I'm very fond of you."

"Fond is one of those words I hate to hear. It's a terrible word."

Now a heavy lorry was grinding past. It sounded like the lorry was in the telephone box with her; but that was impossible.

"I thought the two of you were making fun of me," she said.

He said "I wasn't," and sighed. "Look, I must go. Mr. Turville is calling me over for a rumba."

"We'll come to the hospital tonight."

"Dorothy is taking me home this afternoon."

"See you at home then."

The telephone gave its click and its sad, empty drone. A nurse helped Gary to dress and he appeared to regain some of his good humor as they tussled to squeeze his body into his civilian clothes.

"All set, then," he said, emerging after a twenty-minute struggle behind the screens to stand there, still in his hospital nightshirt and with a raincoat over one arm.

◆　◆　◆

195

There is an art to cheerfulness, but it takes energy. Gary felt his slipping away as he went down alone in the hospital lift. The scuffed aluminium walls reflected his enfeebled face. The whiteness of his plaster cast blended with the pallor of his skin. He wanted to be alone in the lift for one moment, standing there on his own and feeling the jagged edge of the one life he would ever get. He would only allow himself these few seconds.

Gary put his hand out to steady himself and it fell on the Door Closed button, which he held in after the lift had stopped. He heard voices on the other side of the doors but he kept the doors shut. Slowly he lowered his head and sunk his hot wet eyes into the material of his extended upper arm. For a while he stood there like that, crying into the fabric of his nightshirt. Gary had known even before Deborah rang that he had lost her, before he had ever had her. It was a big truth as old as the world that people are losing people they love all the time, and there is nothing you can do about it except cry into your nightshirt. There are no rights or remedies, no ombudsmen, no checks you can write, no relief, no nothing, no Deborah. NoVember.

25th

"They weren't dying, you know. One had an ulcer and the other had something wrong with his ear."

"They must have a policy of mixing up the patients. They don't want a whole ward of bronchitics keeping each other up all night."

"Have you caught anything yet?"

"You'll see, won't you. That's my float on the left, yours on the right."

"And if it bobs up and down it means there's something on the end of the line? Am I right?"

"Well obviously. Try to enjoy yourself, Gary. We're here for your benefit."

"I don't know why they call it a sport, I honestly don't."

"Because it's an activity which gives pleasure but has no bearing on anything."

"And then we throw the fish back at the end of the day."

"That's what the book says. Don't blame me, blame your arm for all this. I'd rather be playing tennis."

"What's made you so aggressive this morning?"

"It makes a change from your aggression."

"Deborah kept her vest on last night, is that it Dermot?"

"Quite the opposite."

"Didn't mine move then? I thought it did."

"It was probably the wind. You've got to admit the countryside is beautiful to look at."

"I've got to, have I?"

"We were lucky my brother lent us all his equipment."

"Yes that was a piece of luck. My, my yes."

"You should have brought Dorothy along and you could have argued with her as well."

"We don't argue any more. We've drawn a line under the past."

"I'll believe it when I see it, this line."

"We sleep much better on the new bed."

"There's nothing better than a new bed."

"Dorothy has to be careful that she doesn't rake my back with her fingernails until it's fully healed."

"Of course she does."

30th

There was general agreement that Geraldine's last get-together had been a flawed event. Gwen, it was remembered, had been told the wrong day. Deborah's participation, it was not forgotten, was prevented because her boyfriend didn't want her to go. Gerald had been called away at the last moment and Geraldine was indisposed chasing her husband down the garden path. Gary and Dermot, who had been able to attend, were willing to try to make a go of it a second time as long as on this occasion they did not have to do all the cooking and the eating.

Deborah, Dermot and Gary came down from their flat upstairs, which they shared. Deborah had brought yellow flowers, Dermot a bottle of white wine from the Moselle region, and Gary a large, flat box of chocolates with a red bow. Geraldine and Gwen welcomed them, standing like bridesmaids at the door, and there was a flurry of indistinguishable greetings as there often is when five people who know each other come together.

Gerald was not yet here but he could be accounted for now, which was a source of reassurance.

November was producing its last rain of the year but it was hardly fierce enough to carry against the windows of the kitchen, where they stood talking in threes and twos. The least established of the relationships was between Gwen and Deborah so their conversations were constantly supervised by a third person.

199

Dermot and Deborah slipped into the sitting room shortly after the uncorking and Gary had pangs which were now familiar to him, of exclusion and jealousy. He had them all the time now that Deborah had moved downstairs to sleep with Dermot and leave her short blond hairs in the bath and sometimes darker ones that curled. Gerald had given Gary one of his early nudes of Deborah and, after a meeting of the members of the flat, he had been allowed to put it up in his bedroom, although Dorothy had once taken the picture off the wall and put it in the cupboard.

Perhaps Gary would move out or insist that *they* move out, or on the other hand he could leave matters how they were because this way, at least, he saw a lot of her, sometimes even her bare legs and underpants as they disappeared into the bathroom. One day he would probably catch her completely naked (it would be difficult to move out until this actually happened) and then another day when Dermot was away she might take his hand, on the spur of the moment, and lead him to her bed (he should stay, there was no point in running away from this situation prematurely). Meanwhile, Gary feared that this evening he was paired with Gwen.

Above the mantlepiece in the sitting room there was a further nude study of Deborah. Dermot still had the tendency to touch her on slender pretexts and now, since by design they were alone in the room, he put his hand into the top of her springy waistband, which held his wrist flat against her stomach. Sometimes she pushed him away. He couldn't imagine the day when he would lose this tendency. He hoped he *would* lose it, because if she ever left him he would be left high and dry with the same obsession to touch and hold her. Deborah had mingled her possessions with his but her trunk had been difficult to accommodate so Gerald kindly allowed her to keep it upstairs in a corner and used it as a low table for his paints and brushes. She had brought new items into Dermot's and Gary's lives—books, a hair dryer, a bathroomful of lotions and oils. They now had two potato peelers.

Gerald entered, discovering Deborah shaking one of Geraldine's bubbles and Dermot with a hand tucked into her trousers.

Gerald was alright now, he claimed (but was he, was he?), and had been given his old job back after the gallery had accepted that he had disappeared only temporarily and for the best of reasons.

"Hello."

"Hello Gerald."

"Hello Gerald."

They had all been invited up to Gerald's studio, as Deborah's old room was now called. Geraldine had been warned to be constructive and indeed managed to be quiet and encouraging on her regular visits to the top of the house. She couldn't help urging him to use more colors, however, and would helpfully bring over tubes of bright orange and blue which he normally refused.

They all gathered in the kitchen again. Gary was being abrasive about the royal family and Gwen became increasingly cross with him.

Gerald still said very little. He often looked over at Deborah. Dermot followed his lugubrious gaze closely. He had been thinking about his landlord recently and suspected that Gerald, the Gauguin of the inner London suburbs who had made his Tahiti among the kiss-me-quick hats and autumnal mist of Brighton, had been keeping his flat there warm for Deborah. Anyone who can see a woman like Deborah posing naked and decide to call her an icon has got to be pulling a fast one. Deborah believed him, but maybe she was being romantic in her cool way.

Gerald would have to be watched. Gary, too, would have to be watched. That was two people. And the man in the sandwich bar who Deborah worked with. Three. There was a lot of watching to be done.

The table in the kitchen wasn't made for six people but by keeping their knees and elbows together they almost gave the impression it was. Gary's plastered limb lay on the cramped table like a fat French bread.

Geraldine led the conversation as they ate—*so, here we all are,* she said twice and implied all the time in the way she looked up cheerily and smiled. She had not recovered all her excitement and vigor but she had had them to excess before; they had driven out the wan, delicate emotions. It had not been all her fault, Gary and Dermot believed; she had always tried to make up for her husband—a dry stone wall of a man— when perhaps what she should have done was to curl up in his silence, sod it.

"Are you alright there, partner?" Gary asked, turning to Gwen.

"Yes," she said, after considering.

"I'm looking forward to the chocolates," he mentioned. The two Geralds were at the sink while Dermot and Deborah were talking to each other.

"Bad for your teeth," Gwen said.

"You know that and I know that," he said, talking into her ear, "but let's not spoil it for the other couples."